Little Red and Other Stories

ÉILÍS NÍ DHUIBHNE

·THE·
BLACK
·STAFF·
PRESS

First published in 2020 by Blackstaff Press
an imprint of Colourpoint Creative Ltd
Colourpoint House
Jubilee Business Park
21 Jubilee Road
Newtownards BT23 4YH

With the assistance of the Arts Council of Northern Ireland

LOTTERY FUNDED

Éilís Ní Dhuibhne has asserted her right under the Copyright, Designs and
Patents Act 1988 to be identified as the author of this work.

Printed in Berwick-upon-Tweed by Martins the Printers

A CIP catalogue record for this book is available from the British Library

ISBN 978 1 78073 263 3

www.blackstaffpress.com

For my friends

Contents

Little Red

A thing Fiona does is online dating.

Not dating exactly. She hardly ever goes on an actual date. But she writes quite a lot of messages to people on a site called Never Too Late. Sometimes the messages are one line long. Sometimes they are just those little smiley things: emojis. You can also send a 'wave' or a 'wink'. Fiona sends a lot of winks, because it's a new experience for her. She has never winked in real life, with her eye, even though her eye is perfectly capable of performing the action and nobody has ever told her not to. Winking. A male thing.

This is how all that started.

A year ago she was flying back to Dublin from a trade fair in Lisbon. It was May, but it had been unseasonably cold, so she was dressed in her winter work 'n' travel clothes. Black with a splash. Black jacket, black trousers. Black boots. (The splash is her bag, which is red.)

As Fiona was making her way to a free seat in the departure lounge, a woman doing the same thing dropped her glasses on the floor, and sighed. 'Feckit!' Fiona put down her stuff, picked up the glasses, and handed them to the woman. 'Thanks pet!'

She was large, the woman who said feckit. Dressed in white trousers and pink flowery blouse. 'You're very good!' Fiona nodded. The woman sat down with a group of companions. Companions who were in good humour and expressed this at a high volume. Fiona sat as far away from them as she could and buried her head in her book – which was not a real book but an e-book. 'I only use it when travelling,' Fiona lied to people – colleagues in the book trade whose lives were passionately devoted to the preservation of the traditional book in the face of competition from non-traditional books and all the innumerable other post-Gutenberg ways of disseminating stories and information. Everyone she knew believed that a book printed on paper and bound in paper or cardboard (not to mention leather) was a precious and beautiful thing, a sacred thing. They all had Kindles but only for travelling (to book fairs and writers' festivals and, of course, ordinary holidays). Actually Fiona uses hers all the time. 'It's just so handy!' But it has disadvantages. It's hard to 'bury your head' in a Kindle, and it doesn't send out the signal at which a real book is adept: 'Do not disturb this reader, who is lost in another world, buried in her book.'

She wasn't lost. Far from it. Keeping her eyes on the screen she eavesdropped eagerly on the woman talking to her friends, regaling them with stories. Cushy Butterfield, Fiona named her, in the privacy of her own head. The name just popped in, from nowhere it seemed, although she knows perfectly well that all names, all images, all ideas, actually come from somewhere, somewhere in the thorny forest of your past, until out of the blue something hacks in and wakes them up.

Often in the departure lounge of an airport, waiting for the flight to Dublin, Fiona's heart sank when she heard the voices of her compatriots. The voices of the Others, the foreigners – their accents, their languages, always sounded beautiful to her ears, light and magical like fairy music. All those lovely words that she didn't understand. By comparison, the familiar flat accents of Dublin fell like heavy rain pounding on the roof on a dark November day. (Is she a snob?) For a while, for a while – until she got used to it again, until their humour, their slagging, cheered her up again, made her feel at home. She didn't feel like that now, not yet. And where did she feel at home? Where she had last felt at home was at home, in her house, with her husband. Unfortunately he was no longer at home. Not at the house they had called home together for twenty-five years. He had fallen deeply in love with someone he had met at a book fair in Slovenia five years ago. It was, he said, a love that couldn't be denied. So ridiculous, so bizarre, so unbelievable. The divorce, solid as lead, had come through earlier this year, five years after he moved to Trieste, where the other woman worked – she is Italian, her name is Lucia, she works in a bank. (So what was she doing at the book fair? 'She's a reader,' he replied. 'You know, Fiona. A human being who actually reads fiction even though she doesn't write it or criticise it or teach it.' Or sell it, like Fiona. He forgot that. Anyway the implication was that Lucia was an exceedingly rare type of human being, worth abandoning your wife of thirty years for.)

On the plane Fiona found herself sitting right beside Cushy Butterfield. What are the chances of that? Fiona had the aisle seat. Cushy Butterfield was in the middle, and a man – Cushy's husband, no doubt – was at the window. At least I'm not in the middle, thought Fiona. She nodded to Cushy, in the interests of politeness, then pulled out her Kindle and continued reading (Rachel Cusk, a sort of auto-fiction novel, the very latest fashion – hybrid car of the written word). She observes the clichéd rule: don't engage in conversation with a fellow passenger until twenty minutes before landing, and usually not then either. She was aware that she missed many good biographical stories but she didn't want to pay the price of those, which could be hearing uninteresting stories for hours, and being expected to offer her own in exchange. Fiona couldn't do that. She possesses stories – who does not? – but it goes against her nature to confide in strangers, and most other people as well.

After about half an hour the crew came around with the food and drinks trolley. She was a little bit hungry. But she couldn't face the cheese and ham panini, the chicken-and-stuffing sandwich. She ordered instead a little bottle of wine and a Ritz cracker with Cheddar cheese – a bargain snack pack. After the food of Portugal – the little custard tarts, the fresh sardines, the wines of Douro and Alentejo – this would taste pathetic. But she needed a break from the book.

Cushy Butterfield got four little bottles of wine, two for herself and two for her husband.

Fiona had never seen anyone doing that before. Most fliers didn't buy the wine at all, these days. They drank their own bottles of water. She felt a gush of empathy for Cushy. A woman who didn't mind passing the time on the plane with a drink, or being mildly outrageous.

'*Sláinte!*' Fiona raised her plastic glass to her.

'*Sláinte!*' Cushy raised hers.

The husband was asleep.

'I'm Molly,' Cushy said.

Fiona introduced herself.

'Were you on holidays?'

Do I look like it? Fiona told her she had been at a conference. Something to do with work. She never liked to tell people what her work was. And, like most people, Cushy was too polite to ask directly. She herself was a teacher, retired. She – Cushy-Molly – had been on a holiday with a group, the Grey Explorers. They had had a great time. She gave the name of the resort where they'd been based – not far from Lisbon. Fiona had been there, on an afternoon's outing, yesterday, with one of the organisers of the conference.

When Cushy moved on to the second bottle of wine, Fiona told her a bit about herself. (She had also finished her first bottle.) 'Get yourself another,' said Cushy. 'There isn't much in these little bottles.'

Fiona had never rung the bell in a plane before, for anything, even though she flies several times a year. But she rang it and got a second little bottle of red.

Cushy told her about a friend of hers, who was a widow. (That's not the same thing, Fiona thought. Being divorced is worse.) But she'd met a member of the trouser brigade on one of the Grey Explorers' holidays last year. 'And now they're living together!'

Yeah, yeah, yeah.

'It's time for you to meet somebody,' she went on. 'That's if you're still interested in the trouser brigade.'

Fiona said: 'I'm sixty-four.'

'Never use the "a" word,' Cushy wagged her finger at her. A? Age. 'Forget it. You're a beautiful woman.'

Some lies are good to hear.

'And he's not going to come knocking on your door and ask you for a date.'

'What do you recommend?'

The Grey Explorers. Or ... one of those online things.

The very next day, as soon as she got up, and before she had unpacked, Fiona signed up for a dating agency. She provided a potted biography, answered a questionnaire about her job, hobbies, age, religion, what she was looking for in a relationship. Set up a standing order: twenty Euro a month, for six months, after which you could cancel it at any time.

That was over three months ago.

She has talked to various men on the phone, and has gone out for a drink, for dinner and once to a film, with three of them. The one she felt she got on best with dropped her politely after two dates. She dropped another quite promising candidate after just one meeting and many phone calls. It's easy to let these relationships fizzle out – they even have a word for it, for dropping someone you meet online and never contacting them again. (The word is 'ghosting'.)

It did seem that most of those she met or talked to wanted more than she did. They wanted someone to replace the wife they had lost, mainly thanks to divorce, sometimes due to death. Someone to go to bed with. Without much delay. That they kissed – however chastely – on the first encounter alarmed her. (Not in a serious way; they weren't dangerous. She just wasn't used to hugging and kissing people she had known for about an hour and a half.)

She quickly figured out what she wanted. Less. Someone to meet for dinner from time to time. Someone to go to the movies with. Someone to go on holiday with. Bed? That would have to be part of the deal, obviously –

although the thought of going to bed with anyone made her squirm. It's one thing when you're twenty or thirty. Forty. But sixty? Seventy? She thinks her body looks okay – although the varicose veins and the fungal toenails are best kept hidden from view, and generally are. But she can hardly have sex without taking her socks off. That's before she starts considering them. The grey-haired men with wrinkled faces and wide smiles. What does the elderly trouser brigade hide in its trousers? Does she want to find out?

Caucasian. Christian. Leaving Cert. 5' 9".

Likes: going to the cinema, music, walking.

Invariably what they are most grateful for is their families, and what they are most passionate about is sport. Mostly what they desire in a partner is warmth, affection and a good sense of humour.

Quite a few of them tick 'maybe in the future' beside the little pram symbol. This is surprising, given that they are to a man aged between 63 and 72 (the age group Fiona ticked when she registered).

The site gave them marks for suitability – good matches. The marks ranged from seventy upwards. Fiona thought eighty-five or so – an A when she did the Leaving – must be good, although it wasn't always clear why (Passionate about: rugby). Then she noticed a few that were graded at 125 or 130. Off the scale. Talk about grade inflation. (Where did it stop? 200? 1,000? But then, why should there be a limit? Who's setting the rules for the dating-site grades?)

A simple comparative analysis revealed that what the men with these Nobel Prize marks had in common with each other and with her was that they were atheists. So that was how the website was evaluating matches. Not on looks, interests, incomes, favourite foods. Smoking and drinking. Religion or lack of it was the key factor, the thing that would unite you with your soulmate. And, when you think about it, that made a certain amount of sense. Although souls, hers or theirs, were the last thing on their minds.

She is running away from a man who might be a policeman. He comes to her house, to arrest her, but she manages to escape. As fast as she can, she runs, and he gives chase. She twists and turns. There are houses, buildings, piles of rubble, bushes, convenient randomly placed pillars and posts to hide behind. (The scenario is based on one of the chase scenes in the detective dramas she is addicted to.) She feels a certain triumph, congratulating herself on her skill in eluding him. She crawls under a car and hides there. She can see his feet, passing, then stopping. He hauls her out and puts her in handcuffs.

In this dream she's not in a version of the house she lived in with her husband, or of the house she lived in with her parents, as in most dreams. She's in something that resembles her new house, the one where she lives now. After the divorce, the family house in Dublin was sold and they split the proceeds. Fiona put her furniture in storage and lived in a rented apartment for a year, which stretched to two years, while she decided where to settle down. During those years, the websites she spent hours on every evening were Daft and MyHome.ie, where you can see all the houses that are for sale in Ireland. She also spent many Saturday mornings driving around looking at houses and apartments open to view. Nothing was quite right. Then history and the personal intersected in the way it often does for people – financially. The economic recession ended. The cost of houses began to rise, slowly for a few months, then dramatically. Places doubled in price. The range of choices narrowed and it looked as if it would continue to do so if she didn't make her move rapidly. In year one of her divorce she had the option of a house or an apartment almost anywhere in Dublin. By year three, it was a small apartment on the northside or a house in a commuter town twenty or thirty miles out. She bought a bungalow by the sea, south of Wicklow town, which, her children told her, was sheer madness. 'I work from home,' she countered. 'There's a train from the town.'

'You'll be so isolated. And what about global warming? The sea will come and wash that house away in a few years.'

'I always wanted to live by the sea.'

Also, it was a nice place for the grandchildren to visit, at weekends. The sea, Brittas Bay, the Silver Strand. The sheep and the cows. (The grandchildren loved it. But they didn't visit as often as she had hoped they would.)

Here she dreams more than she used to in her old house. Something about the fresh air, it must be. Or the silence of the deep country night.

On a rainy morning she sent one of the atheists a message. *Let's meet for a coffee sometime.* Then the rain stopped and she went out to the garden to plant daffodil bulbs.

Now the wind has picked up. There's a storm brewing. She has come in and is sitting on her favourite chair, under the lamp, beside the fire, hugging a cup of coffee. The fire is not lit and neither is the lamp. Her laptop is plugged in but not on. She's staring out the window. Hardly even thinking. She finds she can sit and stare for quite long periods without being bored. It's a thing older people can do. You wouldn't call it mindfulness. Or laziness. She usen't to really understand when older people said, 'I don't have the same energy any more.' But she's beginning to get it. What is this life if, full of care, we have no time to stand and stare. No time to stand beneath the boughs and stare as long as sheep or cows. These lines have been in her head since she was about eight or nine. The poet is saying that the capacity to stare like a cow is a virtue. But is it? Really?

She is staring at something. The apple trees. The long grass – knapweed, montbretia, thistles, grass – that wild stuff. The roof of a house below. The sea. The horizon … beyond, the coast of Wales, which you never see from here although it's not far away.

Sky ever changing, minute by minute it changes.

There's enough going on to keep her idle, sitting and staring, as long as a sheep or a cow.

And then.

A figure appears outside the patio door. He looks at her, and smiles.

Over the past ten or twenty years, everyone in Wicklow, like everyone everywhere, has got big patio doors, the better to see the view. This house is no exception. Now, from inside the house, you can see the whole shebang – fields and sea and sky and sheep and cows. But from outside the house, you can also see everything: the kitchen and living room, the sofa, the TV, the table. Fiona might as well be sitting in a shop window. She could be a plaster mannequin modelling the latest autumn fashions, as she sits there, staring at apple trees.

The man outside could be one of those men who comes to give an estimate on painting the windows, or fixing the TV, or cleaning out the septic tank. It's Sunday, so that is unlikely. But here in the country they can ignore city patterns, they can drop by when they have a minute, when they feel like it.

He is tall, with a long pointy face, a crest of grey hair springing back from his forehead, a sunburnt complexion. Neat clothes – jeans and a pale grey shirt, a grey anorak.

He knocks on the glass. There is no choice but to open the patio door.

Cushy Butterfield was not the first woman to tell Fiona that she should try to get a boyfriend – not that anyone else was as direct as Cushy. Of course there was no such suggestion for a year or two after the departure of her husband. But then she felt there were certain hints, mentions of how so-and-so – other divorcees, widows – had 'met someone'. Conversations about dating websites. It was as if the subtle competitiveness of the teenage years, then the race of the twenties to get a husband, was being replayed all over again, even though she'd passed that exam years before: got a husband, children, a house, all those things you used to have to get to prove you were a proper grown-up woman. Those misogynistic terms, 'on the shelf', 'old maid', had gone out of parlance. But had the attitudes that went with them really gone away? Is a woman alone regarded as deficient in some way? She had signed up to the dating agency because Cushy had been so persuasive. But she had stayed with it for more than one reason.

She opens the door.

Now the sun has come out. There are jokes about the weather, here as in many other places. We have the four seasons in one day. But it was especially changeable this autumn. You had the four seasons in half an hour.

'I'm Declan.'

Is that Declan the plumber or Declan the electrician or Declan the serial killer?

11

'I chatted to you on Never Too Late.'

'Oh yes.'

'You're probably wondering how I got your address?'

There were no addresses or even second names on the website. Or phone numbers. Some members used false names, and didn't even put up a photo – although the advice, from the people who run the site, was that this limited your chances of finding a match.

'A little bit of detective work.' He has an attractive grin.

His accent is vaguely local. She doesn't remember sending a smile or a message to anyone who came from around here.

'Do tell.'

Without being invited, he has edged himself inside, just inside the glass door. She considers leaving it open. Even if she does, will she be able to make a successful dash for it if he tries anything? There are two houses nearby but nobody is in them, at the moment. People come at the weekend, sometimes. Not this weekend.

Then she remembers the other door, which he possibly hasn't seen – the back door. She could go to the bathroom, out there at the back, and escape through that door. If she could somehow get the car key without him noticing she could be gone before he'd realise. That is if he hasn't blocked the gateway with his car – the men who come to fix things usually do that, never considering that she might want to drive somewhere while they are at work. It was a thing she'd noticed, and sometimes wondered about.

'Aren't you going to ask me to sit down?'

'We could almost sit outside.'

Easier to escape, if they are outside.

'Nah. Too windy.' He closes the door behind him and sits on the sofa.

'So, how *did* you find out where I live?'

'I googled you.'

'But that doesn't give my address?'

'I found you on Facebook.' The grin again. 'There are lots of photos of the landscape. And even of the house. The name of the house is on Facebook, on the photo of the gate.'

'Rosamund's Bower.' A ridiculous name Fiona had found in a biography of some Irish writer of fairy tales who lived in St John's Wood in the early nineteenth century. She happened to be reading it when she bought this house. One of the first things she did when she moved was order a nameplate from the hardware store and get her son to fasten it to the gatepost.

'Would you like something to drink? A cup of tea?'

'I'd like a glass of wine, if you have any.'

'Of course … You're driving?'

'Maybe.'

The house is open plan. The kitchen is at the other side of the living room, separated only by a low island. He can see her every move. Unless she can manage to go to the bathroom, she can't get away from him – to phone someone, to text someone, to phone the police. The police! In the town, fifteen kilometres away.

She goes down to the kitchen and takes two wine glasses from a cupboard.

'Red or white?'

This is mad.

'Is there anything to eat?'

'Well, of course. Are you hungry?'

'I wouldn't say no to a sandwich.'

'All right. I was going to eat something myself now.'

She goes to the fridge and has a look. There's some

cold ham, Cheddar cheese. The remains of a stuffed roast chicken. There's also bread which she baked three days ago.

'There isn't a lot.'

'You don't have company? Nobody visiting?'

'No.'

What a stupid answer!

'You like living alone?'

'Well … sometimes. I have a lot of friends in the neighbourhood. People are always dropping in.'

Nobody has ever dropped in the two years she's been here. As she tells the lie, she sees her mobile phone, lying on the countertop. For once her bad habit of leaving things in the wrong places has paid dividends. And luck is with her. He takes his eye off her for a second, goes to the window to look out, so she manages to grab the phone and stick it in the pocket of her jeans. He turns to look at her. She looks at her hands and sort of shakes them in the air.

'I should wash my hands before I start making sandwiches! I've been gardening – they're filthy.'

She'd normally wash them at the sink. There's a bar of soap, and a towel hanging beside the tea towels.

'Gardening in the rain?'

'Yes. That's the only time I can dig the soil in my field. The only time it's soft enough.'

That much was true.

'What did you sow?'

'Bulbs. Daffodils for the spring. And some crocuses.'

'Lovely.' He smiles. He is quite good-looking, for his age, which must be somewhere between 63 and 72, unless he lies about his age on Never Too Late (some of them do, she suspects). She has noticed, on the website, that she usually chooses men according to their looks, even if the website algorithm prioritises religion.

'I love the spring flowers.'

'The bathroom's just here. I won't be a minute.'

He doesn't try to stop her.

In the little hall, she quietly opens the back door – it is really the front door, the entrance door to this house, which has a rather peculiar design. Yes, his car is parked right in front of the gateway, blocking her car in. If she left, she'd have to make a run for it. But she could do that. She could leave and make her way down to the nearest inhabited house, which is about a ten-minute walk. She could hide in the ditch when he came running, or driving, after her. The road is lined with thick bushes, brambles, fuchsia, Japanese knot.

'So you have a door here too?'

He's right behind her.

'Yes.' She is trembling now. Why hadn't she just bolted straight away? Instead of standing there thinking. Hesitating.

'This is actually the main door, even though it seems to be at the back.' She's gabbling on. 'There used to be a bell but it hasn't worked since I ... for ages.'

'You could get a knocker.'

Actually, that's not a bad idea.

'I could put it on for you.'

'Could you?'

'Of course. It's easy. You get one next time you're in town and call me and I'll come and stick it on.'

'The light is gone too. That one.'

She points at the lamp, attached to the wall.

'I'll take a look at that later. It may be just the bulb.'

Maybe he is not a serial killer?

She shuts the door and indicates the bathroom.

'I'll be out in a second.'

15

In the mirror, she sees herself. Her hair with grey streaks – she hasn't been to the hairdressers for a month, she has been considering letting it go grey, or white, or whatever colour it really is under its many coats of fading dye. She's wearing an old blue jumper over a T-shirt and jeans. No make-up.

When she went on dates with other men from the website, she dressed not too up, not too down. She made herself up carefully, and ensured her hair was properly coloured. She had experienced the nervous preparing – the washing, the painting, the selection of just the right outfit – that she used to experience when she was a girl, getting ready to go out on a date with someone she was madly in love with, whose admiration and approval, whose love and adoration, she longed for. In years and years of marriage she had forgotten that feeling. Not that she hadn't dressed up and done her hair and make-up, tried to look her best. But there was no nervousness involved, no excitement. Nothing at stake, unless you counted the admiration of friends, the eternal competition between the women, in the looks department. 'She's looking great!' 'She's lost a bit of weight!' 'What a fabulous frock!' That was something you could take or leave; it was nice, but it was like a boring gift. Like a scented candle, or a bunch of chrysanthemums. Not like first-class honours or the Lottery. So the excitement of the challenge she had felt before those few dates with unknown men had come as a real surprise. It was not unpleasant although it was very stressful. She doubted if she could ever fall in love with any of them. And yet, apparently, their endorsement, their approval, mattered.

She texts a friend. In Dublin. From the bathroom. 'I have had a visit from a strange man. He's probably okay.

16

Ring me in an hour. If you don't get an answer, call the police.'

In an hour? By then she could be a corpse in the boot of his car (it's big, a four-wheel drive). Then she washes her hands, brushes her hair, and puts on foundation, lipstick and eyebrow pencil.

He is sitting on her chair, under the lamp, sipping his wine and gazing out at the sea, when she returns. She puts all the food on the table. The roast chicken and the cooked ham and the cheese. The bread and coleslaw and butter. The bottle of wine.

'Let's eat.'

'Thank you; it looks delicious! Maybe we can go for a walk afterwards, if the weather keeps up.'

'I'd like that,' she says.

Her grandchildren visited her here, for a long weekend, with their parents of course, about a month ago. It had been ages since their last visit and Fiona was delighted that they had come. She did everything to make it a memorable adventure – got new toys, hid a leprechaun (plastic, hideous) in the long grass. Made good food and brought them on picnics. Told stories.

Since the eldest, Ellie, was six months old, Fiona has been telling her the story of Red Riding Hood, and many others. She told Red Riding Hood most often because Ellie had a lovely Red Riding Hood doll, that you could turn inside out and upside down, that could be a granny, or a wolf, or Red Riding Hood herself. Fiona always told the traditional story that ends with the wolf being slit open by the woodcutter, and the granny climbing out of his stomach.

But this time, Ellie wanted a different version. (She used the word 'version'.) 'Tell me the version that's not scary,' she said.

'What happens in that?' Fiona asked.

'The wolf doesn't eat the grandmother.'

So Fiona told her. At the end of the tale, the wolf and the grandmother and Red Riding Hood all sat down at the kitchen table and ate the stuff from the basket.

'Is that it?' Fiona asked, when she'd finished.

What was the point? Where was the story? And who had put such ideas into Ellie's head? That's what Fiona thought. It is not a proper story. No tension. No fear. No loss. No relief.

The key thing is missing.

But Ellie had nodded, apparently perfectly satisfied with what she had heard.

Blocked

At eleven this morning, as usual I phone my mother. Bronwyn. I have called her by her name, her unusual name, since I was a teenager. For the past few weeks she has answered the phone when I've called and said, 'No, I'm busy.' But today the phone returns an unusual sound. Bip Bip Bip. Then that stops.

Blocked. My *mother* has blocked my number.

It surprises me that she knows how to do this. She's reasonably competent with technology (although she has stubbornly and irritatingly resisted doing certain by now elementary online tasks, such as signing up for online banking) but sometimes the stereotype of the little old lady who hasn't a clue about technology takes over, blocks out of my memory my knowledge that she sends WhatsApp messages, uses Skype. Watches plenty of films on Netflix. She doesn't have an iPhone but that's just because she prefers her laptop, for the moment.

I phone my brother, who lives closer to her. I'm fifty miles away, across the border, but he lives in Monaghan, not far from Tubbernashee. He can drive quickly to the house and check up on her, even if she blocks his phone number – I don't think she will, but who knows? She is liable to do anything at the moment.

Not that she is crazy, or mad. But she is not herself – which means, when I think about it, that she is someone else. Isn't that a very strange expression? Not herself. If not, then who is she?

When I was not myself as I now am, but a younger version of that, forty years ago, I attended the nearest secondary school to Tubbernashee, which was, and still is, in Milltown. Milltown is eight miles from our village, and a school bus picked me up every morning at eight fifteen – the bus had to stop several times on the way to school, at the end of many lanes and boreens. The school was a big modern building, built at the end of the sixties after free education had been introduced. Before, the children who could afford to go to secondary school had to go to boarding schools – Monaghan, Sligo, Dublin. Then only a few children went to secondary. But by the end of the sixties everything had changed; everyone was going and they had to extend old schools and build new schools to accommodate them all. Ours was one of the brand-new ones. By the time I was attending, there were a few hundred pupils in the school, boys and girls. Milltown, a pretty enough town straggling up the side of a steep hill on the edge of a lake, was a busy place already, but the new school gave it a boost of energy, a sense of importance. Even though it was unlikely that schoolchildren would be among its customers (perhaps they had expectations of the teachers?) the hotel painted its big hall door a bright modern colour – orange. It used to be black. It was a handsome grey stone building with peachy-coloured roses rambling around the porch. You'd catch a comforting smell of roast meat, coffee, as you passed the door, with its gleaming brass knob and knocker, always wide open during the day – affording a tantalising glimpse of polished wood, a crystal vase of hothouse flowers, red carpet.

After free education, the shops, too, seemed to stand up straighter, smarten up. There were several of them, for clothes and hardware as well as the usual butchers and bakers and grocers. Three hairdressers. Pubs galore. A mart once a month. Now Milltown is close to derelict. There's a butcher, who survives by selling the best local meat (organic – but it always was, I am pretty sure) and also the things tourists like to buy: local honey, home-made blackberry jam, little sachets of lavender. (We get a few tourists around here, especially in mid-July. People from over the border come to escape the Orange parades.) All the other shops closed gradually, over the years. When Lidl opened on the road outside the town the stragglers put up the shutters. The noble old hotel has been for sale for about twenty years. It's falling down. Soon the roof will be gone and that'll be that.

I seldom go to Milltown now. But back then, I was very familiar with the town. At lunchtime, my two friends, Nora and Evelyn, and I would wander up Main Street. Nora, whose father was a teacher in a little primary school in another village, generally had money for chips. I had a sandwich – cheese or ham – wrapped in the shiny waxed paper sliced pans came in then, or in a paper bag, and Evelyn something similar. Nora never shared the chips, since they were her lunch, and we accepted this, even though the smell of them could drive you to the brink of insanity. But I could put up with the torture, because once a week, on Fridays, I had money for my own. So did half the school. That meant we would spend most of Friday lunchtime standing in a queue in The Pronto. (It never occurred to me to hold on to the money and get chips on some other day, when there would be no queue. It didn't occur to anybody else either.)

On Monday, Tuesday, Wednesday and Thursday, when there was no queue, Nora was in and out in minutes and we had plenty of time to spare since we got an hour and a quarter for lunch: pupils who could went home for their main meal – potatoes, slices of fried mincemeat, peas. Or sausages and potatoes and beans. Fish or eggs on Friday. Dinner was served in the middle of the day still, in the country. But we couldn't go home for lunch so we spent most of that time wandering around and looking in the shop windows. There were two drapery shops. Watters' sold everything – children's clothes, flowery overalls for old ladies and the other kind of thick blue overalls for farmers. That wasn't very interesting. Emily's Boutique was. Its owner, whose name was Madge, sold jeans and expensive tops. Short fashionable frocks, dramatic shoes – sling-back stiletto heels. In the autumn, she filled the window with long gowns for the debs' balls – which were introduced to our town around the same time as the free education. Red silk, white muslin, black satin. In spring Madge displayed bridal gowns. Naturally we spent a lot of time examining what was on offer there, and deciding what sort of bridesmaids' frocks, and wedding dress, we would choose. I was for a princess style, and my bridesmaids would wear pale green. Evelyn favoured mermaid, with pink, and Nora – already plump – was going to go for a modern slinky style in cream with royal blue bridesmaids. (In the event, cream is what she chose – she married before any of us, the year after the Leaving. We should have been the bridesmaids, in royal blue, but she didn't have any. It was a quiet wedding.)

I also liked to look in the window of McArdles, the hardware shop. There were thousands of objects in that window. It was said that Mrs McArdle put things in, forgot about them and never took them out again; that there were ornaments and objects that had been sitting in the window for fifty years, gathering dust. Teapots, vases, sets of fancy wine glasses. Pictures of little girls with big dogs, little girls with little dolls, little girls weeping from enormous round brown eyes. A food processor. A sewing machine. Statues of plaster and plastic, some holy, some not. There were so many things in the window that there was always something I had not seen before, no matter how often I looked. This I found intriguing – because often the thing I hadn't seen had obviously been there for ages. I engaged in this particular bit of window shopping on my own – Nora and Evelyn weren't interested in McArdles. I don't know why, but I was addicted to that window.

I was standing there, pondering the use I might have for a blue willow pattern china milk jug and sugar bowl in my future life, when somebody touched me on the shoulder, and requested that I go back with her to the school.

Somebody.

Mrs McCarron, the French teacher. The thing she had to tell me was that my father was in the hospital. The tractor had turned over on him, as he was collecting bales of silage from the hill field. He was already dead when she tapped me on the shoulder, but she didn't tell me that. It's possible that she didn't know.

My mother. Why was she called Bronwyn? Everybody in the county was called Eilish, or Sheila, or Winnie, or

Mary. Annie was the most popular name of all. Well, the reason for her name was or would become commonplace. Her mother had seen a film in which a character was named Bronwyn, and she fell in love with the name, and insisted on it … although actually she had to register her and baptise her as Mary. Mary Bronwyn. Because Bronwyn is not a saint's name and the priest insisted that it was against the law to give a child a name that was not a saint's name, and her mother believed the priest, as people tended to, back then. This was in the forties. Of course he was wrong, there was no such law and lots of children were named after characters from mythology. Deirdre and Grainne and Fionn and Ronan. He would have had to accept those names, and wouldn't have questioned them, because they were from Irish myths and legends. Welsh was another story. The Welsh names sounded more exotic than Grainne or Deirdre. They sounded more pagan. Also, they sounded like the names of fashion models, or film stars, which is probably what worried the priest.

I always think that Bronwyn lived up to the glamour of her name. Like most people, she lived in a small enough house on a small enough farm when she was a child, and then she married my father, and they bought a rundown house in the village – rundown, but quite big and potentially handsome, an eighteenth-century house with long multi-paned windows, built of important-looking grey granite blocks. He was able to do up the house, bit by bit, because he was a carpenter. There was a good deal of work for carpenters then as always, especially a country carpenter whose skills were not confined to woodwork. He could do almost anything related to repairs or building. Like most country carpenters he was also a small farmer – he looked after his family's little farm in a valley three or four miles from the village, on the other side of the hill. In short, they were ordinary people, with not much money. But Bronwyn, who had a special name and now a special house, behaved as if she herself were special. She dressed quite well, every day, whether she was at home doing the housework, or over at the farm milking the cows. She had a hippyish look. The long floaty skirts of that time. Soft blouses, with granny-print patterns. In the winter, big loose sweaters in bright colours – orange, electric blue – over her jeans, or black polo necks and black jeans. Her hair, fair, was long, and she often wore it in a thick plait. Sometimes she wound the plait around her head in a rather fairy-tale style: a Bronwyn style. She looked different from the other mothers. And the thing she did which was really unusual was to have two children. Me and my brother, Ken.

How did she manage that? Everyone had big families. The era when people routinely had ten or twelve or fifteen children was over, even where we lived, but most families ran to four or five. Contraception was still illegal in Ireland. In cities, women – and more often men – got hold of it anyway and for us it would have been relatively easy, with the border fifteen miles away. But old habits die hard and in our county people were very religious, very law-abiding when it came to the teaching of the Catholic church and the Presbyterian. (Less so where the laws of the land were concerned.) What made their insistence on clinging to dark rules that made life tough for women and gay people and others so difficult to understand was that they were, they are, always very kind people, I like to think, naturally kind and compassionate. As time goes on I have been trying to reconcile this aspect of their nature with their conservative, rule-bound religious attitudes –

up there, they haven't kept pace, for the most part, with the liberalisation of Ireland. My theory is that they stick to what seem to be bad, cruel, ridiculous, rules because they have very vivid imaginations. They were, and possibly still are, genuinely afraid they'd go to hell if they stepped out of line. Most other people seem to have successfully given up on their belief in hell, even people who believe in 'an afterlife', a word that has a life of its own, no longer attached to the traditional image of a golden palace in the sky. When people say, 'There must be an afterlife', what I think of is butterflies. Don't ask me why.

My parents may have been exceptions. They were exceptions in other ways. They had what we would now call 'a good relationship'. Better, it seemed to me, than the relationships of a lot of the neighbours, where the husbands and wives didn't seem even to talk to one another, ever. (Although presumably they must have exchanged a few words, when they went to bed and conceived yet another child.) My dad gave my mother – and us – a goodbye kiss every morning when he was going out to work, building houses or other things, or going to the farm. They sat together in front of the telly in the evenings, occasionally discussing what they were watching during the ad breaks. They were friends.

I don't know how she – it would have been her doing – managed the birth control. I could ask her, obviously – if I ever got to talk to her again. But it would not be easy. It's never easy to talk about sex, as some writer I read sometimes has written. These days they talk about it a lot on the radio, and in the papers, but I'm not so sure people find it easy to do in real life. Listening to the radio is one thing.

*

When Dad died, Bronwyn didn't fall apart. She didn't cry, ever – at the funeral, or at any time. At the wake, and at the afters – which were in the hotel in Milltown – she behaved like a practised hostess, as if she had been doing this all her life: shaking hands, accepting condolences, offering people cups of tea, asking if they had had a sandwich. She didn't need to do any of this, apart from shaking hands – neighbours and my father's sisters were managing all the hospitality, guiding people to the buffet, pouring tea when the waitress forgot or went off to do something else. Bronwyn could have sat on a sofa in the corner, doing nothing – it was expected that the widow would, that we would sit with her.

After the funeral, my dad's sister stayed with us for a week. Helping. Guarding? We didn't go to school – although I would have liked to. I would have liked to get back into my own life.

But I was expected to spend all that week with my mother, comforting her, grieving with her. The last thing in the world I wanted to do.

I devoted all my energy to getting away from my mother. It wasn't easy.

First, as often as I could, I shut myself into my bedroom and read. Since the school year had just started I had a few new books – we were doing *Pride and Prejudice* and *Hard Times*, so I read both of them. I didn't really like *Hard Times* – it's possibly Dickens's least entertaining book – but I had nothing else. No question of going to the library in Milltown. That would have looked bad.

When I got tired of *Hard Times* I went out for a walk. Not a thing I did much under normal circumstances.

Once, Bronwyn offered to come with me. 'I could do with some fresh air,' she said.

I pretended not to hear.

Off I headed, alone, along a narrow road behind the house. It wound around through bumpy hilly fields for about two miles, then joined another boreen that came back to our village by another route. Six or seven miles.

The weather was lovely that week. Mild, sunny. It never rained. The ditches were laden with blackberries. I could smell them, that sweet musty bramble smell, a smell I always longed to catch and keep in a bottle. I ate plenty of berries, as I walked along. I relished them. I knew that it was unseemly to enjoy berries the week after my father died. I knew I should be refusing food, starving.

This laneway was very dense, very green. Heavy oak trees, sycamores, beeches in the fields. The ditches with their blackberries, lingering orange lilies, other flowers I couldn't name then – knapweed, vetch, herb-Robert. (We didn't give names to flowers. My father had known the names, in Irish, because his father had come from a place in Donegal where they spoke Irish. He used to tell me the names when I was little. But for some reason the only one I could remember was méaracán gorm: blue thimble. That was his name for the bluebells, or the harebells – there were still some in bloom, now in mid-September.)

The blackberry walk lasted about three hours. Then there was another I could take – a bleak lonely road over a drumlin. Now there were no fields, just heathery hillside, bog cotton – such a feathery, strange flower, if that is what it is, like cotton wool. It always gave a twitch to my heartstrings; it looks so bleak and lonely, like the souls of dead babies, or their little white garments on a windswept clothes line.

When the thought that I should be at home with my mother crossed my mind – which it usually did, when

I saw that bog cotton – I brushed it away. She had my aunt for company (she didn't like her much). And Ken. He was at home. Yes, but – as I was well aware – he spent his time watching TV, and refused to talk about what had happened, or about anything, then or ever. One of the emotions that assailed him, and me, among all the others, was a sort of shame. We were embarrassed that our father was dead, had died in a stupid accident, when all the fathers of our friends were alive. And as well as that, I was embarrassed by our mother's sadness. I knew she was 'going through' something, that for her the death was worse than it was for me. Much worse. But I didn't want to face that thought.

For me, the idea that my father didn't exist any more was impossible to grasp in any real way. When I tried to catch the thought – to get my head around it – it slipped away, like a fish from a flimsy net. Back into obscure waters, another world. All I could do was walk and walk and walk, as far as I could from the house. That crucible of huge unexpressed emotions.

Wakes, candles, prayers, funerals. Tea and sandwiches and whiskey. A circus. To hide what had happened, to carry some people through the gap. Those rituals are for the people who are not really affected.

Not for my mother. She wanted to find words, to talk. 'I'm in another world now,' she said to me. 'How will I manage, without him?'

Tears. Oh, how I hated my mother's tears.

'You'll just have to,' I said.

Such cruelty. She meant how would she go on without his companionship, his love, his support, all that. Obviously. Another world. But she was in another world financially too. I was fifteen, Ken twelve. We were neither of us going to finish school and get jobs in a shop or a factory, even if such jobs existed to any extent. We didn't want that and neither did she. The era of the children dropping out of school to become breadwinners, 'to help out', was over, thanks to the free education and so on. So my mother, not we, would have to go out to work.

She was in luck. A solicitor in Milltown had a vacancy for a secretary. (There were still solicitors in Milltown. A Bank of Ireland. A Garda barracks. A dentist. All those signs of a living town.) Mr O'Hare. My mother could type – this seemed to be the main requirement for any secretarial job. Like most people, she could also answer the phone, and welcome clients to the office and ask them to wait. Find old magazines to put in the waiting room. Receptionist duties. In addition she was reasonably good-looking and well-dressed – also a requirement, understood although not articulated. And she could drive the car – an old Opel – and get herself to work.

In the middle of October, just four weeks after my father's death, she started her job. She could now give me a lift to school, if I wanted it, since she started work at the same time that school began. But I had the option of the bus – it was free. At first I said I'd stick to the bus. However, since that meant leaving the house half an hour earlier than my mother, I was soon taking her up on the offer, as was my brother. But we came home on the bus since she didn't finish work until five thirty.

It was around this time that I stopped calling her mammy, and began using her name. Bronwyn.

Bronwyn enjoyed working, as far as I could tell. She transformed herself. She'd always dressed well but after six months 'in the office' – which is how she always described her job – she looked almost like a different person. She had her hair cut, and its natural browny fair lightened, and she got highlights. She stopped wearing midi skirts and floral blouses, Laura Ashley-type frocks. She had worn black anyway after my father's death – she said it wasn't a gesture towards tradition, but that she felt more comfortable in it. She went on wearing black, never went back to her flowery ditsy clothes. Usually she dressed in black trousers and jacket, with a white blouse or a silk top in some rich jewel-like colour – deep pink, rust, dark ochre. She had some chic slim skirts, an alternative to the trousers, which she wore with boots and black tights. She now looked younger than she had when my father was alive, and much smarter. Soon my pals started wondering when she would marry again.

But she didn't. She had a few boyfriends – men friends. They never came home with her but she went on dates – dinner, at the hotel in Milltown or a restaurant in Monaghan, Saffron, which was her favourite, or a film. I don't know if the option of marriage came up for her – there weren't as many eligible middle-aged men around then as there are now, thanks to divorce coming in. Her relationships could last for a few years, but never for longer. In fact, I wonder if my mother was behaving the way men used to, in the old days. She liked dating, but she ran away from commitment? Fear of commitment, they used to call it, in the agony aunt columns. She didn't mind being committed to seeing a man for dinner regularly, going to the movies. But apparently she didn't want another husband. Anyway she had a commitment. To me and my brother. We were company for her, around the house.

That ended, inevitably and soon enough. I went to Dublin to college. I got a grant – it wasn't enough to cover the costs, by a long shot, but she was able to give me some support, and I worked right through the summer holidays and also at weekends, at a club in Leeson Street, to pay rent for the house I shared with five others, and to buy some food. First I was a waitress and then I was promoted to the grade of hostess: I met people at the door, guided them to a table or seats, and took their order which somebody else – the waitress – delivered. The tips were good. Sometimes enormous – rich people came to the club, politicians, people whose faces I recognised from TV. That was where I met my husband. A medical doctor, ten years older than me. He was, in fact, divorced – they had divorce in the north of Ireland long before we had it. One night he came to the club when he was down in Dublin at a conference organised by some pharmaceutical company. After our marriage I moved to his city, Derry – mostly people moved in the opposite direction during the Troubles but his practice was up there. Derry wasn't far from home anyway – about a hundred miles up the A5. I could see my mother at weekends, if I wanted to.

In fact, I tended to visit about four or five times a year.

And that was okay. Because after I'd married and moved away for good, my mother had acquired a very close friend in the village.

Pat Gallagher. Or 'Patsy, as I prefer to be called by those I deem close friends.'

Patsy lived down the street from us. Her husband – and she herself – owned a shop, which was a bit like McArdles in Milltown, only bigger. It was a needle-in-a-haystack shop and sold absolutely everything. Fishing rods, microwave ovens, china and delph. Mousetraps. Chocolates and cigarettes and cigars. Tweed jackets and scarves from the handweavers in Donegal. Ordinary clothes. It had been the Gallaghers for generations and it was a fabulous shop. They also owned the town garage and car showrooms, and a pub.

Pat was not local – she was from Glasgow. Glasgow was the place most people from our district emigrated *to*. Glasgow, or Canada. The thing about the Glasgow ones was that they came back on holidays. Every summer, when I was a child, there were several families home for the holidays in our village. They always seemed better off than we were – they would come in rather nice cars, and they had new sparkling clothes, white socks and sandals. After a day – or an hour or two – of initial shyness, they would blend in with us, the locals, and we would have great fun, playing street games, going on picnics – I remember one family, the Fergusons, which consisted of four or five children, driving about a dozen of us to the lake, three or four sitting in the boot of the car.

She had been one of those kids. As sometimes happened, she fell in love with a local boy. In this case, one of the eligible Gallaghers, who owned the shop and the garage and the pub. Not a local who would ever have to emigrate. On the contrary – she was the one who immigrated, to marry him.

Pat belonged to a different social class to my mother. Even in that little place, with such a tiny population, there was a hierarchy. We had a beautiful house but it was on the village street. No family from the bourgeoisie would live there – they all lived in big villas, surrounded by manicured gardens, rich with hydrangeas and roses and agapanthus flowers, on the road overlooking the lake, with its cluster of islets, scattered like soft green cushions on the calm water. A perfect view. The Gallaghers lived in the biggest of these houses, with large bay windows, a wide balcony, and three or four terraces of lawn that looked like thick emerald carpet descending to the water's edge. They would have associated with the doctor's family, to some extent with the teacher's, with the owner and manager of the flour mill. And with the solicitor's, which is how Pat came in contact with Bronwyn. They encountered one another at a garden party he – the solicitor – and his wife gave, one August, after race day in Rathmeen. Race day was something everyone went to; I – and I am pretty sure Bronwyn and no doubt many others – found it invariably disappointing and boring. Crowds of people walking up and down the street, licking ice-cream cones or eating chips. Some races, and unintelligible announcements over big loudspeakers, those big horns, attached to telephone poles. 'Competitors for the Monaghan Breeders' Cup assemble now at the starting line. Donkey Derby will commence at four o'clock.'

A garden party would have been a godsend.

They had, of course, a marquee, in case the weather was inclement.

He introduced my mother to Patsy. I imagine the conversation went like this.

'Oh, I believe I have had the pleasure of making your acquaintance previously!' Patsy talked like someone out of a nineteenth-century novel. She was addicted to the works of Charles Dickens, Thomas Hardy, and George Eliot. 'I've seen you frequently in the shop.'

'Aye, surely,' said my mother. She was dressed up in what she supposed was appropriate garden party gear: one of her old Laura Ashley skirts, white, with a blouse of blue and white stripes. And a white straw hat.

'What a charming ensemble!' Pat bounced and twirled. Her face, her body, were in constant motion. A live wire. You could hardly pin down what she looked like. But she made an attractive impression – curly dark hair, a short red frock, red high-heeled sandals. 'Most imaginatively coordinated, if I may say so.'

'Oh.' My mother prepared to dismiss the compliment, as she always did any compliment – to say she had the skirt for years in the back of the wardrobe, which was true. But she didn't get a chance.

'Nice but not gaudy, as the monkey said when he painted his tail blue!'

Bronwyn didn't get a chance to respond to this comment either. Pat didn't allow for interruptions or answers when she was in full flow. Bronwyn wondered if she were drunk. (She was.)

'Isn't this a delightful gathering? So impressive! And they do it annually, every race day without fail. Where does the energy come from, I ask myself. Especially with that daughter of theirs. Special needs. Some would say a blessing and others the opposite. For my own part, I am on the fence. I am not blessed with offspring, of any shape or form, special or needy or commonplace.'

My mother knew about the daughter, but not that the party was an annual occurrence. This was the first time she had been invited, although she'd been working for Mr O'Hare for ten years.

'And now I am going to request another glass of champagne. It is excellent and so refreshing on this exceptionally warm day. No, do not restrain me. You shall have one too. You look as if you need several.'

She tottered off on her high heels across the lawn to the table where the drinks were.

My mother didn't make a decision to avoid Patsy Gallagher in the future, but only because she didn't think there was any necessity for such a decision. She assumed that after the garden party people would return to their assigned perches on the social ladder, and she and Patsy would never meet, except by accident on the street or in the Gallaghers' shop, where they would exchange greetings and move on. But a week after the garden party Patsy knocked on Bronwyn's door. And they got on. She became a frequent caller, gradually a confidante, a firm friend. She became the friend and neighbour Bronwyn badly needed, now that she lived alone most of the time – Ken was working in Monaghan. (He could easily have commuted from home but for some reason he chose to get a gloomy little flat in the town and stay there.)

Bronwyn continued to have the occasional man friend. Patsy had her husband, of course. But they didn't have children, and, it was rumoured, he was a drinker. He managed the garage, and the shop, during the day – most days. In the evenings he was often in his own pub, although he had two barmen looking after that for him. He was not behind the bar but in front, chatting and drinking.

Patsy didn't see much of him, apparently. I don't know how she spent her evenings. At home, drinking wine and reading novels? (She was a reader, all right.) Watching TV.

My mother would have been doing the same. While she was still working, she and Patsy met for lunch in town. At the weekend, Patsy called to the house; they drank tea, they went for walks. When Bronwyn retired from the solicitor's office Patsy was in and out almost every day, as far as I could gather.

It let me off the hook.

I visited more often when my children were older. Every couple of months or so I went down for the weekend, sleeping over on Saturday. (Longer than that I never stayed in my mother's house – she came to visit us, for a week or two weeks at a time, and for Christmas, of course. And once a year we went on a little trip abroad, somewhere easy – Bruges, Bath, Edinburgh.)

Patsy popped in for coffee when I was there but didn't linger. I didn't like her much. I think that's true. Apart from the obvious flaws – she never stopped talking, she could be mildly malicious, and her style was pretentious and ridiculous – there was something else about her that I couldn't put my finger on.

'So your sojourn in Bruges was satisfactory?'

'It's beautiful. We had a great time.'

'I had the pleasure of visiting Brussels once for a wedding. If my memory serves me correctly the groom was a third cousin of Jack's, who had some inferior position in the EU. I must say I never ate more disgusting chips in my entire life. And they insist on bragging about them as if they had invented the chip!'

'We loved the chocolate, and the little coffee shops.'

A cafe like a doll's house, with delicious coffee, china, flowers and perfect small cakes, overlooking a canal. Lace. It was like my vision of something created from the objects in the window of McArdles shop.

'Chocolate! Yes, I acknowledge the superiority of the Belgian chocolate. It can be purchased in a shop in town. I often submit to the temptation. Leonidas I believe it's called. I am especially partial to the praline.'

Her quaint style was something I – and everyone – got used to, and enjoyed up to a point. You need some eccentrics, out in the country. But she had another habit, a way of making conversation that lots of people practise. She took the account, or the idea, that the person she was talking to had said, and added something to it. 'Bruges is gorgeous.' 'Oh yes, I had the pleasure of visiting it.' Or 'So is Brussels.' It's a natural way to expand a conversation. But some people overdo it; they do it all the time. Anything you have done I have done better. Or at least as well. Patsy was one of those. Irritating.

She also had a habit, unconscious I am sure, of taking other people's ideas or opinions and offering them as her own. Well, Bronwyn's ideas, or mine – I don't think I ever met Patsy in company with anyone else. Not even with her husband. They had been married for decades but they were hardly ever together, at least in public.

'Do they sleep together?' I asked Bronwyn.

'How on earth would I know that.' Her answer was predictable.

But she knew, I am pretty sure. She knew more than she let on.

My mother fell.

This happens, when you are eighty.

It happened in an unusual way though. Not a slip on ice or a trip over a cable. She was sitting on her sofa reading, which she did for hours every day – in her retirement she became a great reader and drove to the library a few times a week to borrow books, and DVDs, which she watched in the evenings. She had a tendency to sit with her legs crossed, or sometimes with one leg tucked under the thigh of the other. She stood up. The foot that had been tucked under was asleep, deprived of blood flow. Down she fell on her wooden floor and broke her leg.

No phone close by.

Patsy found her, when she called in the following day. She phoned me, of course, but also phoned an ambulance and got her to the hospital, where she stayed until I arrived. She was enormously helpful. She was a life-saver.

I hugged Patsy before I hugged Bronwyn.

It was a broken leg. Nothing life-threatening. My mother came and stayed with us in Derry for a few weeks. Then, although she was on crutches and in a plaster cast, she wanted to go home. Patsy would look in on her, she said, and there was talk of a nurse or home help. I phoned every day and drove over to visit twice a week, on Wednesdays and Sundays. Ken dropped by occasionally, if asked to do so. (I was the one who did the asking. My mother didn't like to make demands on Ken.)

I was used to hearing friends talking about their elderly parents, reporting how difficult it was to look after them, about the lack of support (from the authorities, the health system, the other relatives). About how stressful it all was. It was understandable. It is stressful. But reading between the lines, you got the impression that these people were secretly longing for their parents to die, so they would cease to be a burden. Few seemed to enjoy spending time with their parents – or, more often, their parent, more often, their mother. The pattern was that the women looked after the men, who died first, and then the grown-up children would be left to cope with the mother. As far as I could make out, it was at this point that the family home changed from being a place the adult children liked to visit occasionally to being the last place they wanted to be.

This leg episode was the first sign of Bronwyn's vulnerability, the first major indication that now she was definitely in the ranks of the elderly, that she was about to metamorphose from being an independent adult, who could be called upon for help, to the opposite: a needy old person – a burden.

But it didn't happen. Bronwyn did not become an old bag, a hag, a witch, an irksome burden.

Not this time anyway.

She was always glad to see me when I visited, which I did much more often now, but I had no sense that I was necessary – even though she could walk only with difficulty, and could not, for instance, drive her car.

'It's very good of you to drive down here and see me,' she said. 'It's lovely to have time with you. But you don't need to come so often.'

It was the opposite of what other elderly mothers said to their daughters, according to what I heard. According to what I heard, what elderly mothers did most of the time was make unreasonable and petulant demands on their exhausted children and complain that they didn't visit often enough, or for long enough. What elderly mothers specialised in was making their offspring feel endlessly guilty and inadequate.

Bronwyn was different, maybe because she had been widowed for such a long time? She had learnt to be independent under difficult circumstances?

'I like coming to see you,' I said, which was true. Now. Especially after that statement of hers. 'I feel I should be doing more for you, actually, while you're recovering.'

'I'm fine. I'll let you know if I need help.'

I brought flowers, and made sure the dishwasher was empty. I took laundry and did it at home. But the fact is there was never much to be done. The house was neat and clean, as it always had been. More than that – it looked fresh, as if the blue-and-white checked curtains had been newly washed and ironed, the furniture polished. As if someone was spring cleaning it.

I didn't say what I thought – that she was exceptional,

amazing. That she was a mother in a million, different from all the others.

And she didn't say what she knew, which was that she didn't need me, because she had someone who was more than willing and able to help.

Patsy.

Patsy spent two or three hours a day with her, cleaning, running errands, cooking. Fetching books from the library, discussing the books with her. And, it turned out, a year later, withdrawing all my mother's savings from her bank account.

The businesses Patsy's husband owned, the shop and the garage, had become redundant over the years. Nobody needed a shop like theirs for clothes or paint or food – everyone drove to the big new shopping centre in town. There were big filling stations and garages there too. Of course, a filling station will never go out of business completely; people always need petrol in a hurry, and a local pump is a most desirable service. But somehow even though everyone knows this, most of the time they fill up at the big stations in town where the petrol is a few cents cheaper. Eventually, like most of the filling stations in the country villages, Gallagher's had to close. The pub had never been much more than a hobby and with the new drink-driving laws, it collapsed.

None of that should have been disastrous for the Gallaghers. They'd run a successful business for a long time, they had money. They had quite a lot of money. However, Patsy's husband decided to introduce something new, something that the area needed.

Broadband.

He was right about the need for it, and the demand. But what he didn't understand was the complicated politics involved. He wasn't a member of the party that dominated the local council. He was never going to get the contract to supply the region with what was now regarded as an essential service by everyone – and the second coming, as far as rural Ireland was concerned, by many. (Broadband would save the country from emigration, unemployment, crime, youth suicide, if you believed what you heard from campaigners on the radio.)

It might have been regarded as the salvation of rural Ireland, but it bankrupted the Gallaghers.

I found out what had happened when Bronwyn was considering getting an accessible shower downstairs. The bathroom was upstairs having been put in by my father long ago when it seemed more elegant and sophisticated to have upstairs bathrooms, because most houses around here had them tacked on to the back downstairs. She got an estimate and accepted it. The bathroom installer – a local who sometimes called himself Heavenly Showers, and sometimes Mick Conlon – required a small deposit before he started work. Cash. So Bronwyn went to the bank – she didn't do online banking, that was one of the new things she didn't do – to withdraw money.

There was none. The money in her savings account had been transferred, in instalments of one thousand Euro at a time, to her current account, and then withdrawn from an ATM using her debit card.

Patsy.

When Bronwyn broke her leg, Patsy had kindly offered to get cash for Bronwyn from the ATM from time to time. Bronwyn had given her her card, her PIN, her account details. I don't quite know how Patsy had figured out how to do online banking for my mother and to get into her account, but she had, and she had taken all her money.

I called the police. Patsy was arrested and charged with fraud. She was tried and given a prison sentence of two years, one suspended.

Bronwyn has been refusing to talk to me when I phone. Now she has blocked my number.

Of course, I don't take this lying down. I drive to Tubbernashee and let myself into the house. I don't have to knock, I have a key. Luckily she hasn't changed the locks – well, she wouldn't, she couldn't, because that would cost money.

(Of course she has *some* money. Her widow's pension, and the small pension from her job with the solicitor. Barely enough, hardly enough, to live on in the most frugal way. What she doesn't have is her considerable savings – the nest egg she could rely on when some emergency occurred, when she needed or wanted something new. Including, actually, even new clothes.)

Getting into the house doesn't help much.

Bronwyn is there, all right. She is sitting in an armchair in the living room, watching TV. Her handbag is clutched to her stomach.

'I'm here!' I say.

No reply.

'Would you like a cup of tea?'

No reply.

There is no reply to anything I say.

And, two weeks later, the locks are changed.

Bronwyn refuses to talk to me, or to my brother, since Patsy's trial, and sentencing.

We don't blame Bronwyn for what happened. We understand. I don't know why she has cut us off, shut us out of her life.

I am assuming that at some point, when she becomes ill, has another fall, or needs something, she will make contact. Now there is no Patsy to take care of her. She'll have to depend on us.

Once – years before my mother broke her leg – I came down to see her on her birthday. A surprise visit – often I just sent something, made a phone call. But I had time. And yellow roses and a cashmere sweater. It was a glorious day in early October. Blackberry season still. I thought, we'll go for a walk in the lanes, pick some berries. Then out to dinner somewhere.

She was in the living room, with Patsy. Not in the embrace of love. Nothing so dramatic. They were sitting, one on each side of the fire, logs blazing in the old fireplace. The room was warm, and rich with the scent of carnations. My mother was reclining in her chair. Patsy was reading in her lively, melodious, undulating voice, her lovely Scottish accent.

> 'Micawber!' exclaimed Mrs. Micawber, in tears. 'Have I deserved this! I, who never have deserted you; who never WILL desert you, Micawber!' 'My love,' said Mr. Micawber, much affected, 'you will forgive, and our old and tried friend Copperfield will, I am sure, forgive, the momentary laceration of a wounded spirit, made sensitive by a recent collision with the Minion of Power—in other words, with a ribald Turncock attached to the water-works—and will pity, not condemn, its excesses.'

Patsy did the voices. She was a natural actress. My mother started laughing.

> Mr. Micawber then embraced Mrs. Micawber, and pressed my hand; leaving me to infer from this broken allusion that his domestic supply of water had been cut off that afternoon, in consequence of default in the payment of the company's rates.

Bronwyn laughed and laughed. She went into a fit of giggles, the kind teenage schoolgirls can have. Uncontrollable, laughing till it hurts. The kind of laughing you seldom experience after the age of fifteen or sixteen.

She saw me standing on the threshold with my armful of yellow roses. She waved, weakly, a welcome.

But the laughing didn't stop.

Nor could.

Lemon Curd

'I'll cut the bollocks off your mother.'

The voice is a man's. Loud. Angry.

Miss Moffat hears a lot of interesting mobile phone conversations on this bus. For example, just the day before yesterday, a young man – nice-looking, neatly dressed, obviously on his way home from work – asked someone, 'So do you want that pony?' Pony? The word intrigued her. Miss Moffat had a feeling that it might be a slang word for some sort of drug. But she wasn't sure. She considered the possibility that he was referring to an actual horse. 'I'll see you beside the garage at eight' had been his next line. You could have a horse beside a garage, or even in a garage, out in the western suburbs to which this bus would eventually find its way. Pony could be a little horse, or some sort of drug. The transaction of dubious legality in either case.

The voice of this man, today's man, is so angry that she is afraid to look too closely at him. Crazy people don't appreciate being looked at, even though they are inviting stares. She saw him getting on the bus, though, and waiting to pay his fare, or more likely show his free pass to the driver. You could hardly fail to see him. He is dressed all in black – black hoodie, black jogging pants, one black shoe. He has only one foot. His right leg stops at the knee. Something about the way he is dressed suggests (to her) that it has been cut off, and not by a doctor and not long ago. The bottom of his trouser is wrapped around the place where the short leg ends; it looks like something packed in a shopping bag. Under his oxters, two big crutches. Before he made his threat, to somebody's mother, or to her mother, or maybe to everybody's mother, she felt sorry for him. But now she mainly feels frightened.

He comes down the aisle, repeating his threat, and sits down beside her. Not exactly beside, but just across the aisle. Nevertheless, he's very close. Just two feet separate them. And she doesn't like the look of those crutches. While he was walking – hobbling – they inspired pity. Now, when he's sitting down, with the crutches sort of resting in his lap, they look like weapons. Don't be silly! He can't do much harm, him and his one leg. No. The thing is, standing, he can't do much harm. But from his seated position wouldn't it be easy to pick up a crutch and hit someone with it? The nearest person to him, for example, who happens to be Miss Moffat herself.

'I'll cut the bollocks off your fucking mother!'

This is the third time he's expressed this rather strange intention, since Miss Moffat's mother, even if she happened to be alive, which she is not, had never had bollocks. Could it be that he's mixing up the word 'bollocks' with something else – breasts, for instance? Boobs would probably be the word he'd use. But that word sounds too harmless and comical.

Who knows what he's talking about? The language

of this part of the city is still foreign to Miss Moffat. 'Bollocks' might have more than one meaning, over here, on the northside? Miss Moffat is used to hearing words for sexual organs bandied about by angry men on some of the dodgier streets in the inner city. The words of choice refer to female organs (although not boobs). Anyway, now it's not so much 'bollocks' as the word 'cut' that bothers Miss Moffat.

She makes a snap decision. Get off the fucking bus. (She's picking up the local dialect, without even trying.) There's another one right behind, so she could hop on that. No time lost. She'll have to pay again. But her life is worth two euro fifteen cents.

She's on her way into town to her lesson in Russian. For over a year she has been taking classes in this subject, chosen because she needs a hobby, in her retirement, and because she likes Russian writers, by which she means Chekhov and Tolstoy. Turgenev. (If there are any Russian writers who haven't been dead for over a hundred years, she hasn't heard of them.) She is into her second year of study and there is no possibility of reading these writers in the original, and she doubts that she ever will. So far, all she can manage are the short pieces in the textbook, about somebody buying a hat in a hat shop – not a thing she has ever done, but maybe they still have hat shops in Russia – or going to the doctor, or checking into a hotel. Miss Moffat can ask a Russian stall holder in the bazaar for a kilogram of apples or potatoes. How much does that cost? Thank you. Goodbye. And she can do some complicated negative interrogative sentences involving lots of finicky little particles that need to be placed in the correct order, for instance: Will you not put on your trousers tomorrow? But she hasn't got much further than that. It is a difficult language and she tends to forget things. A year ago she knew how to get out of bed and wash herself and get dressed, but they have moved on to another textbook. It is almost two years since she encountered knives and forks, plates and cups. Now it is about flying from Moscow to Madrid for a conference about the internet. There is a lot of stuff about social media, its good and bad points, how it affects the youth of today. A bit on museums, galleries, places of historical interest pre-revolution. You start off in the kitchen, bedroom and bathroom, as in life, but soon you progress to museums and conferences. The words go in one ear and out the other. Miss Moffat toddles along, scattering Russian words, long and short, to the wind.

To get anywhere, it would be necessary to go to Russia for a month or two, live with a family, immerse herself in the language. Miss Moffat doesn't think she is brave enough to face a Russian family (or any family) for two months, or even two weeks, much as she desires variety and believes herself to be a good traveller. She has recently moved from the south to the northside of Dublin, for instance – apparently a journey that very few people make in their lives.

They come across the word for criminal in class today. *Prestupnik.* The teacher explained that it is based on the word *stup*, meaning step. (Good. Easy to remember then. Some of them are like English words or French words, though most are not.) A criminal is someone who oversteps the mark, who goes too far.

'What a brilliant word!' says Miss Moffat.

Of course it's written in the Cyrillic alphabet, in which all words look more important. **Престъпник**.

She seizes the opportunity to tell the class she met a criminal on the bus, on her way into town. Short digressions are permitted, ideally in Russian, in the interests of conversation practice.

'He was on something, I suppose.' She says this in English. 'Dublin seems to be full of men on something these days,' she adds. Men who are full of anger, and shout about it to the world at large.

The teacher asks her to explain what 'on something' means. His English is excellent but he doesn't know all the idioms. Then he suggests a few ways of saying 'addicted' and 'drugged', in Russian. He agrees that there are a lot of loud and aggressive men in Dublin. It is almost as bad as Moscow, in that respect, and that surprised him when he first came because the other cities he knows, New York for instance, are much quieter. But he disagrees that the man on the bus was a criminal. The real criminals don't shout at random people on the bus. They keep a low profile.

This makes sense, Miss Moffat agrees, although privately she wonders. Maybe that's the way things work in Moscow and New York but around where she lives she's not so sure. The dodgy types she meets on Dorset Street seem proud of their lawlessness. They flaunt their aggression, like the heroes in ancient myths. Look at me, I'm stronger than you, I could kill you if I felt like it, they seem to proclaim, as they swagger along the street in little groups, or glower at her from derelict shop doorways. And anyway, how did that guy lose his leg from below the knee? She's seen the movies, she reads the papers. She knows what the gangsters get up to, how they deal with people who can't pay for their drugs.

Miss Moffat plans to walk home after her Russian lesson but when she comes out it's raining, so it's back on the bus. On Upper O'Connell Street, through the window, she sees a man grabbing a woman. Oh, roughly he grabs her. The woman is young, a girl, and she's cycling on the wide footpath. The man grasps her shoulders and shakes her. Even though what he's saying is not audible from the bus it's easy to read his body language. He's objecting to the girl cycling on the path – which is four metres wide. He's shouting 'What the fuck do you think you're doing? Who the fuck do you think you are?' (She's guessing. Every second word is 'fuck' at this end of the street. Their vocabulary is quite limited.) He's pointing at the bicycle. After a while he shakes his head angrily and stalks off, in the huff. He's a short man with black hair and a bird face, with a black moustache. A black T-shirt. He thrusts his head forward, like an angry bull, as he strides down the pavement.

Framed by the window of the bus, the scene is a bit like the cartoons without words presented in the Russian textbook. The student is asked to write the dialogue. These cartoons generally depict someone buying vegetables (or a hat), or catching a train. They don't involve *prestupniks*. Even if there are a lot of angry men on the streets of Moscow, they don't make their way into textbooks called *Russian for Foreigners* Book A2.

The girl gets back on her bike and cycles on. There are not very many pedestrians on the path; the street is thick with traffic, buses and cars and trucks. No cycle lane. In Dublin, you are not allowed to cycle on the pavement – it's not like other European cities. The angry man had the law on his side. But what the girl was doing made sense, if her aim was not to get run down by a bus or a truck. And it's not legal to grab people by the shoulders and shake them either.

Miss Moffat moved to her new apartment a few months

ago. On a whim. Her mother, with whom she had lived all of her life died. The last years were difficult, to be honest. Miss Moffat had lived in one house for her entire life. James Joyce lived in about twelve places in Dublin before he left and lived in goodness knows how many more in other parts of the world before he died. Yeats likewise. (Miss Moffat was an English teacher; she knows things like this.) Even ordinary people, teachers, for example, or civil servants, usually managed to live in two or three different places in the course of a lifetime – a lot more if they were from down the country. I'd like to live in at least one other place before I kick the bucket, she thought, and explained to people who thought she was off her rocker and asked why. Spain – Spanish was her other subject – was a possibility. They would have understood Spain. But eventually she bought this apartment in a very nice area close to the city centre, on the northside of Dublin. People – in Greystones, but also in her new neighbourhood – seemed to find the choice astonishing. It was generally assumed that she must be 'from here originally' and had come home to die. She moved in August.

The first morning is fine and sunny. Birds are singing in the bushes around the apartment block. Miss Moffat wants to have her breakfast on the balcony. It does not get the sun in the morning – this is an advantage; it's better to get the sun in the afternoon. But it's such a calm lovely day that that does not matter. No milk. She can't take her coffee without milk. Well, of course she can, but she doesn't like it and this morning, the first morning, she wants to enjoy her breakfast.

She tidies herself up a bit and goes out, to the supermarket, which is less than five minutes' walk away. So handy! Worth moving just for that really! It's a good-size supermarket, and, wide awake after the walk in the sunshine, she takes her time, going around slowly, selecting fresh crusty bread, a good French cheese, as well as the milk she came out for in the first place, and a tub of yoghurt. Of course she doesn't know where anything is, since she has never been in this supermarket before. She has to go up and down nearly all the aisles.

She turns into the one where she thinks she'll find honey. It is the sort of summer's day on which you would like to eat honey. And on the shelves are several kinds, manuka and clover blossom, Irish and imported. But she also sees something she loved when she was a child, and hasn't tasted since then. Lemon curd, in a cute little heart-shaped jar. Into her basket it goes, with the bread and cheese and milk and yoghurt. Then, around the corner comes someone she hasn't seen for years. An old boyfriend, from whom she split up when they were both nineteen. He became well known later, in the arts world. He's an actor, mostly on the stage but also in television dramas. So she knows his face, even now. Most people know it.

'Hello!' she says

He doesn't return the greeting. Instead he makes a face, he scowls, and he hurries his way up the aisle, his head thrust in front of him like an angry bull.

She stops in her tracks, in front of a stack of chocolate spread and peanut butter. She's shaking, and she feels that lightness in the head that comes before you faint.

Does he live somewhere around here? He must. Who but locals would be in the supermarket at nine o'clock in the morning?

When he was a student, of law, he belonged to a bunch of people who fancied themselves, who believed they were the Irish answer to Oxbridge students. And in fact lots of that bunch have gone on to be politicians, judges, important media figures, that sort of thing. They spoke in the accents of the best south Dublin suburbs, as Miss Moffat did herself, though she spoke less than they did, and not so loudly – the girls were quieter than the boys, and they didn't take part in the weekly debates that were a key part of that life, as the boys practised for the parliament, court room, the television studios. The girls were on the social committee; they sat at the side of the stage, wearing long evening dresses, and when the debate was over, they made tea and sandwiches. Poured the wine, when there was any.

There was a thing all of that crowd did to people they didn't like, or had fallen out with. They gave them the cut direct. He explained the phrase to her. When you met an enemy, or someone you believed was inferior, you pretended not to see him or her. If they looked at you or greeted you, you ignored them completely. 'You pretend they don't exist. It's very effective.' They had to practise the cut direct, these ambitious boys and girls, as they trained for their future as leaders of the country.

When Miss Moffat and this man had broken up, she did not use the cut direct, or any sort of cut. She explained to him, over coffee, that she was going to Spain for a year, to perfect her Spanish, and that she thought it was a good time to take a break. From him. She knew they would remain good friends. She would write to him and she hoped he would write to her too.

He stood up and left the table, without a word. She never heard from him again. Occasionally, over the years, she had bumped into him – in a bookshop in the week before Christmas, at funerals. He always pretended not to see her – gave her the cut direct. In the early days her letters were not answered – and the letters were not from Spain, but from Greystones. Three days before she was due to travel, her mother had tripped on the stairs and broken her leg. Miss Moffat had no choice but to cancel her plans and stay to look after her. By the time her mother was back to herself, almost five months later, it was too late to go. Miss Moffat applied for a job in a school in Bray and got it. That's where she worked until she retired.

He isn't using the cut direct now, though – that icy, controlled ignoring, no doubt developed in England. The corridors of Eton and Oxford, the royal palaces. You're out of favour. Off with your head. Now he looks more Irish, more northside Dublin. Hot and furious. He looks as if he would like to raise his fist and strike her in the face. He thrusts his head down, like a bull's. The last thing she sees is his backside, in expensive black jeans, as he storms out of Jams and Condiments into Coffee, Tea and Biscuits.

Miss Moffat collects herself, tiptoes down to the checkout, and escapes. She decides not to let it bother her. Really, the nerve of him. The fucking bastard, as they'd say around here.

On the bus (she's still on the bus, from Russian) while she's busy remembering, someone starts to sing. It's a female voice, soft and tuneful, and she's singing in a foreign language. Not one Miss Moffat can name. She sings and sings. Miss Moffat would like to see who is producing the singing but she is too polite to turn around and look. On the DART, which she used to travel on when she lived on the southside, people occasionally got on and sang or played a melodeon and then went around with a hat, collecting money from passengers. Romanian, they were, always.

Miss Moffat begins to think of her old home. She can easily transport herself to it, in her thoughts – walk around the rooms, go out to the garden, or the street. Every detail of the house is firmly imprinted on her memory. The shining maple floor. The white walls, the bookshelves, the old paintings. The pear trees, the hydrangeas, the view from the front window. She remembers the texture of the grass that she cut so often, and the ancient pink roses. There is not a cranny of that house that she cannot revisit in her mind any time she wants to. But as yet she has not gone back to the actual house, or to the road. For some reason she is afraid of doing that, that the sight of it, the real bricks and mortar, grass and trees, will overwhelm her.

The song is over. The singer passes down the aisle to get off the bus. She's a small well-dressed girl, better dressed, in Miss Moffat's opinion, than most of the young women on this bus. She can't quite put her finger on it but they all share a certain style that is different from what you see on the other side of the river. Mostly they wear black leggings, and little jackets, leather or denim. Many are rather plump. Their faces are smooth as china, coated in thick make-up and they frequently have very thick black lines drawn around their eyes, so that they look a little like badgers or those American animals – raccoons. But this girl is trim and pretty and has a proper knee-length winter coat – a lovely coat, blue wool, with velvet-covered buttons and a velvet collar. She could be from Greystones or Blackrock or Killiney. She steps lightly off the bus and walks away in the rain. Will no one tell me what she sings? Her song was sweet, though, not plaintive at all. A song of joy, or simple pleasure? Even if of old forgotten far-off things?

At nine o'clock she watches the news. A man has been arrested on suspicion of murdering a twenty-seven-year-old woman in an apartment on Manx Road.

The next road to hers.

She wonders if the murderer is the man with one leg. Or the man who grabbed the cyclist by the shoulders and shouted at her. Or the cutter direct. The details of the case will gradually emerge. She'll find out in due course.

The chances are that it is none of those gentlemen, the ones she has encountered recently, those oversteppers of the mark. Her mark anyway.

But goodness knows.

It could be any of them really. But the victim could not be the girl who sang the song, the girl in the blue coat with the velvet collar. Not her. Not a girl with a voice like that, and a coat like that, that would not would not look out of place on a five-year-old princess from Greystones or Killiney.

These are Miss Moffat's thoughts as she sits in her new apartment, watching the nine o'clock news.

Just as an image of rich dairy cream being poured over a juicy apple pie appears, the ad that signals the end of the news and the start of the weather forecast on RTÉ, the doorbell rings.

It is a long ring. Long. And loud. An aggressive ring.

Nobody ever rings her doorbell, nobody who hasn't telephoned in advance.

Miss Moffat doesn't answer. She switches off the light. She is about to turn off the TV too but changes her mind. Then she goes into the bathroom, bolts the door and steps into the shower. Fully clothed. Hiding.

There's a spider in the corner. An enormous spider.

Before she moved, long before, one of her old colleagues, who was a mine of curious facts, told her that the biggest house spiders in Ireland are to be found on the north side.

So it's true.

She remains in the shower for half an hour. During that time the biggest spider in Ireland goes back down the drain.

Miss Moffat goes to bed.

She tries to sleep.

She hopes to swoon into a sweet, a lovely dream.

White Skirt

'Your white skirt.'

Auntie Annabel had a white pleated skirt that she was very proud of. She referred to it often, in a tender proprietary tone, as if it were a cherished pet, or even a child. 'My white skirt.' Her voice was always breathy and excited, suggesting that life was full of pleasant surprises. She wore the white skirt with a sleeveless silky top of a delicate rose colour, a string of pearls and pearl earrings. But this happened only once during her two-week holiday. The white skirt was for very special occasions and there hadn't been any – the one outing it had got was to Mass on her first Sunday, so people would get to see it.

Now it was time to pack her suitcase, a large cream case with two blue leather bands around each end and two shiny brass locks. We were in the front bedroom, which was where she had stayed during her holiday. The cream cardigan, the pale blue mohair jumper, the striped blue and white cotton frock were all arranged on the bed, as tidy as if displayed on a shop counter. But the white skirt, her most treasured garment, was still in the wardrobe.

'You little dote! Wouldn't I have gone back without it and where would I be then? You're so observant!'

'Observant.' That wasn't a word anyone in my house, or anyone in the area, would ever use. I had to guess what it meant. But I guessed right. I was watching her every move with great attention. That's what it meant. And this was a thing I loved to do. I loved watching grown-ups as they went about their activities, and even more I loved listening to their conversations, even though I didn't understand what they were talking about half the time and usually as soon as one of them noticed me standing close to them, with my ears cocked, they shooed me away as if I were a chicken or a dog who had strayed into the house from the back garden.

Like a lot of our aunties, who were really cousins, or sometimes just friends, Auntie Annabel stayed in our house when she was home from England for her fortnight's holiday. We had a spare room. Our house was not big but there were only two of us, me and my sister, whereas most families at this time, in the 1950s, extended to five or six, ten or eleven if they lived down the country. (One of our aunts had fifteen children.) Auntie Annabel came to Dublin to visit her parents, who lived in a small flat in the next parish to ours – she got the bus every day and spent most of her time with them.

Her parents, Mr and Mrs Surrey, were very small people, old and bent. They both wore tiny gold-rimmed glasses on their small pointy noses, and had thin soft grey hair. Mr Surrey always wore a grey jacket, and Mrs, fluffy beige cardigans. Grey slippers on their feet. They were gentle and kind, and I loved visiting them – we went four or five times a year, up the stairs to their flat, which consisted of three miniscule rooms on the first floor of a house in one of south Dublin's old leafy squares.

They would give us strange but delicious things to eat – a deep red jelly made with port wine, and little macaroons with cherries on top. They offered sherry to my parents, in dark red glasses, and also to us, but my mother would let us take only a tiny sip. Mrs Surrey would be distraught if she had no lemonade or stone ginger beer to give us instead. She would not have had any warning that we were visiting – none of us had a telephone. The custom was just to call on people whenever you wanted to, although I suppose some notice was taken of when they would be likely to be at home. In the case of Mr and Mrs Surrey, that would have been almost always, except on Friday mornings when they went to collect their pension from the post office and do a bit of shopping, and, of course, Confession on Saturday evening and Mass on Sunday morning.

Unlike most of the other aunties, Auntie Annabel was unmarried. She was Miss Surrey. She worked as a nurse in Manchester. She was much prettier and more glamorous than most of the other aunties too, and she smelled lovely. Smooth blonde hair to her shoulders or pinned up in an elegant plait, neat figure. 'She is petite,' my mother – who was not – said. All her clothes looked as if they had just come from the cleaners; she pressed everything before she put it on. 'Pressing' was her word for what we called 'ironing'. I tried to spot the difference. It seemed to have something to do with care, attention and speed. Pressing was a slow, loving activity, whereas ironing, at least as carried out by my mother, was fast and impatient. In her hand the iron shuttled up and down the table, up and down, quick as a train. And my mother had the habit, which I have inherited, of not bothering to iron bits of garments that wouldn't be seen – she just did the collars and sleeves of our blouses, for instance, since the rest of them would be tucked under our gymslips, out of sight. During the ironing sessions, which happened once a week on Thursdays, my sister and I were stationed beside her; our job to fold the clothes and stack them on a chair, ready for putting away (we would also have to do that). We did a lot of housework, when we were eight or nine – as well as folding the ironing, we washed the dishes after dinner, and polished the brown linoleum on the hall floor every Friday afternoon. We carried out these tasks dutifully but not well and with deep resentment. Nevertheless, visitors were impressed.

'Aren't they so *good*?'

I hated being called 'good' in this way. The voice – of Auntie Annabel – was admiring, but tinged with pity. She felt sorry for us. That was humiliating. The children she knew, the children of England, where she and all the visitors came from, would never dream of doing these chores, or be expected to. That didn't surprise me. The children of England who came to visit us were a superior breed, to me and my sister, and the children on our road. They had lots of smart new clothes, and regular pocket money with which to buy sweets. They got comics every week, and were laughed at when they said something that would have been defined as cheeky by our parents. They were, as an entire population, spoiled, according to my mother, who didn't conceal her dislike of the representatives of English childhood who came to stay with us. But I liked them very much. I wanted to be them.

Auntie Annabel and my mother had long chats over breakfast. We all ate breakfast in the scullery, at a small table covered with a blue oilcloth, but Auntie Annabel had hers in the dining room, at the table by the long window. The table was covered with the white linen tablecloth. Before going to bed it was set, often by me, with the good china, the fine cutlery, the sugar and jar of marmalade, for the morning. She would have half a grapefruit, a boiled egg or sometimes a fry, and tea. The window looked out over the back garden. A big plum tree that never bore fruit and was eventually cut down grew just outside, and we could hide behind its trunk and spy on her through the net curtain, sitting in her white satin dressing gown. My mother would join her for a cup of tea, almost always. Coming up with replenishments – a fresh pot of tea – would give me an opportunity to hear what they were talking about, if I played my cards right.

Other people, always. Mutual acquaintances, relatives. Or sometimes people only known to one of them, but of special interest for one reason or another, characters plucked from life to illustrate a fable or moral tale. There were rich pickings in the neighbourhood, and in our extended family.

Auntie Rosaleen, for example. Annabel's sister, married to Uncle Phillip. They too came to visit us, regularly, with their daughter Diana, a princess of a child with long wavy hair, big blue eyes. Auntie Rosaleen looked a bit like Auntie Annabel in that she was small and bird-like. But her colouring was completely different. She had dark hair, brown eyes, glamorous tanned skin. Her favourite colours, in clothes, were brown, fawn, cream – shades that set off her looks perfectly.

She worked as a secretary in a solicitor's office. (They both had better jobs, higher status jobs, than most of our other relatives. The uncles in England worked on the buildings, mostly, and the aunties had jobs as dinner ladies, or nurses' assistants. Rosaleen and Annabel had gone to secondary school.)

Rosaleen had been engaged to an Irishman. This was in the story. Long ago. A year or two after the War.

'One of the solicitors?'

No. There were no Irish solicitors in Manchester – Auntie Annabel was quite firm on this score. The man Rosaleen was engaged to worked on the buildings. Of course he was a foreman, a manager, not an ordinary builder, the implication being clear. Mick Cronin, from Cork. A very nice fellow. They were going together for nearly two years when they got engaged. The deposit was down for the house, the chapel was booked, and the hotel. And then.

Auntie Rosaleen was walking down the street one Saturday afternoon, and who did she bump into but someone she had been doing a line with before the War, just after she came over. To England, that is. She couldn't have been more than sixteen or seventeen. They were great together, as we used to say. But then off he went to the War. He was in the Navy. She was to wait and she did. When the War was over there was no sign of him. The thing is he had stayed in the Philippines for a few years and she had heard no more from him. She didn't know if he was alive or dead.

Or married, interrupted by mother.

This remark was ignored.

She met Mick at the club. And they got on. Well enough. He hadn't much to say for himself. Nobody would call him good-looking but looks aren't everything. Are they?

No. No.

He was a hard worker. Mick. Michael. He had red hair, a sort of crew cut. Anyway. One day after she bumped into her old boyfriend on the street she went around to Mick Cronin after Mass and called off the wedding. The invitations had already been sent. They had to be unsent. And six months later she married Phillip.

Uncle Phillip.

'What happened to Mick?'

Auntie Annabel didn't know. He was no longer in the story.

Phillip Burton was. And this story was not over, because Phillip was English and Protestant. Not even from Manchester – he came from some village in the south of England, Adelstrop, somewhere nobody had ever heard of. So. Needless to say, there were frowns and sulks at home. Mr and Mrs Surrey were not happy; they weren't friendly to Phillip, at first, when he started visiting. They didn't know what to make of him, with his shapely English face, his posh accent and gleaming brown brogues. If it hadn't been for Diana, who was born very soon after the marriage, they would never have accepted him. But they had to see their grandchild.

'I suppose they got used to him. You can get used to anything.'

This was the most interesting story. More often, the conversations focussed on illnesses of one kind or another, fatal ones taking priority. Lumps like turnips, unbelievable pain leading to death.

'He screamed with agony. "Don't take me there, don't take me there!" he shouted, when they were bringing him down to the operating theatre for treatment. This was in the Meath Hospital. But they'd take him, of course, and he'd scream his head off afterwards, with the sheer pain.

Poor Paul. It was a mercy when he finally died. Sometimes you do have to wonder.'

That was my Uncle Paul, who lived in a big house not far from us, which he had inherited in some complicated way from the doctor who used to live there. It was an elegant house with a flight of steps up to the hall door and a long back lawn, velvety green, dotted with rosebeds, like a park. He filled this lovely house with divan beds, for boarders. All men, who worked in offices or shops or were going to uni, as it was called then. 'The boys.' (He said 'byes', the pronunciation in his dialect, which I despised in those days.) Uncle Paul tramped around the basement kitchen of the house, in a stripy apron, peeling potatoes, frying rashers, washing dishes. His soda bread was fluffy and irresistible, his apple tarts sweetly perfect. 'He has a light hand with pastry!' my mother said, and my father, who never lifted a finger in the house, would roll his eyes to heaven. Paul cultivated the back garden, pruning the roses – sometimes he gave us a bunch, crimson or cream or peachy, velvety petals with a rich fragrance you could bury your whole life in for a minute. He did all the housework himself until at some point one of the 'byes' stayed on and gave him a hand. Peter: a youngish boy with a round chubby face, pink cheeks. Peter and Paul! More rolling of the eyes from my father. But in fact my father seldom if ever saw either of them. We visited on a weekday, my mother and we girls, after school or during the dreamy summer holidays. And Paul never came to see us.

'And you heard what happened when Paul died?'

Auntie Annabel shuddered slightly , because in England everyone said 'passed away'. Never 'died'. Even I, aged nine, had observed this.

'No?'

'Everything was left to that Peter fella.'

Their eyes locked. Not another word was said on the subject.

'She was so worried about the pain in her breast. Terrified.'

Bridie, Annabel's cousin. She lived in Wexford.

'Did she go to the doctor?'

'She claims that she did but I wonder. You'd really have to wonder. Because do you know what it was?'

'What?' My mother puffed on her cigarette. She smoked a little – a cigarette with her cup of tea, four or five times a day. There were a few ashtrays in every room, as in most houses then.

'Her bra.'

This was quite interesting.

'I said to her, "Can you open your blouse?" We were in the kitchen but there was nobody else around. So she unbuttoned it and took it off. Because I had my suspicions. And there it was, the bra, an old one – I'll spare you a description of what it looked like. Four sizes too small for her, at the *very least*. Digging into her like a … like dog's teeth. Or … shackles. Manacles.'

I didn't know what manacles were.

'"We're going to Cassidy's right now and fitting you for a new bra!" I said. "I won't take no for an answer." She couldn't afford a new one, herself. Needless to say.'

'How many have they now?'

'Nine. And number ten on the way.'

My mother shook her head.

'I gave her a bit of advice on that side of things too.'

'Hm.'

'Well, you know yourself.' She paused. 'We can get …
preventatives.'

My mother took a drag of her cigarette, thoughtfully.

'In England.'

'I've no doubt.'

My mother stood up. She was stiff with something.
Annoyance, or anger? She saw me, standing by the door,
and clipped me on the ear, and shoved me out of the room.

Auntie Annabel brought us to the zoo, on her last day
in Dublin, and, as she hugged me and said goodbye, she
pressed a half crown into my hand.

And that was the last time she visited us. We continued
to call on Mrs and Mr Surrey, once or twice a year, for a
while. My mother would ask after Annabel and Rosaleen
and Diana, and we would be told that they were well, but
not much else. After we children had eaten our purple
jelly and cream and drunk our ginger beer we went out
to play on the street anyway, so we missed a lot of the
conversation.

Other aunties and uncles and cousins came to stay with
us, in the summers and at other times. As I got even more
observant I saw that an uncle would slip an envelope to
my mother, as they said goodbye, even as the auntie would
press a coin – a shilling, a florin, a half crown, depending
on their generosity – into my palm and my sister's. Later,
as we moved up into teenagehood, this pattern of visiting
stopped. Grandparents died, the English children grew
up. If the aunties and uncles came over, they didn't
stay with us. Maybe they could afford a real B&B? The
seventies. It wasn't yet the norm to stay in a hotel, unless
you were really rich. But maybe the custom of staying

with aunties, for your holidays, of coming home from England, was starting to die out. These changes don't happen overnight.

We grew up too. And we moved in quite a different direction from the English cousins. That was the direction of college, degrees, higher education. It seems that all that floor polishing and dishwashing had been leading to another kind of life altogether: a life of study, of exams, to a middle-class existence. I don't think that is what my mother had in mind when she made us fold the shirts. She'd perhaps been training us, in case we had to get jobs as housemaids, or housekeepers, or as housewives. But as it happened the habit of doing chores meant we knew how to apply ourselves, and so we did reasonably well in school, and at exams, including the scholarship exams which started when we were eleven. In addition, my mother was adaptable and allowed us to take advantage of new opportunities. Free secondary education, free university education. They came along in the nick of time, and we availed of them. The English cousins, to a person, started working straight out of school, as we progressed to BAs and MAs. PhDs. There was no stopping us, and it all seemed to roll along naturally, as if we were in a canoe on top of a wave that carried us farther and farther away from our roots.

Well, in a way.

Of course there were only the two of us in the canoe.

Not that all the education led to anything spectacular. But it led to a life that was very different from our parents', or our aunties'. We didn't work in shops or as dinner ladies, even as secretaries. And we didn't go to England.

Except now and then. As tourists to see things my mother never knew about. The V&A. The Tate. Stratford-upon-Avon. Or, more often, on work-related things, to conferences.

I was at such an event in a museum in Manchester. This was when I had a job in a museum in Dublin as a curator of historical collections. I took the opportunity to explore a bit of my own history – it was the eighties, and I had many ideas then, about different kinds of history, official and unofficial, herstory and theirstory, children's history, that sort of thing. It was all becoming popular; things were changing in the way historians looked at the past, in the way museum curators decided what objects were worth collecting and preserving.

Now it occurred to me that I could explore some of my own past and perhaps use it in some way in the museum. I'd no idea how but that was one of the ways I worked – creative research, I called it. I decided to look at the places where my aunties had lived. I'd never seen their homes. An aspect of the childhood visits that looks odd now is that they were all one way – the English relatives came to us in Ireland, but we never went to them. It was a question of money but it was more than that. We had no desire – our parents had no desire – to go to England. It didn't cross our minds to cross the Irish Sea, since we didn't have to. The idea was you'd only do that if you were forced to, in search of a job. My mother's picture of England was of one large ugly city, without a tree or a field or a river. In her imagination, and in mine when I was a child, it was an utterly bleak urban jungle – not a place anyone would voluntarily visit, for pleasure. When we went on holidays, which in due course we did, it was always to the west of Ireland, Kerry or Clare or Donegal. The wild Atlantic, the land of heart's desire.

I did not bump into Auntie Annabel as I walked down

the street. Such chance encounters can happen, but they don't happen very often. I snooped around the area where they lived, Salford. It was a lot less salubrious than I had expected, than the clothes and style of the aunties would have led me to expect. Street after street of small brick houses with bay windows. This type of place was getting trendy back home. The place I had grown up in, where my parents still lived, had become fashionable. But this didn't seem to be happening in Salford, not at this point anyway. Maybe there was just too much of it, too many streets of the Edwardian or Victorian houses? Too close together, too Manchester-y.

I didn't bump into anyone I had ever known. But I passed Auntie Rosaleen's house. 197 Cliftonville Road. I had written the address so often on Christmas cards that it was imprinted indelibly on my memory. When I saw the number on the house I hesitated for a second or two. But I was adventurous then – full of confidence; I had got my PhD, I had married an academic, I had what people considered an interesting job, although when I was cataloguing objects in the museum it bored me stiff – a task that is a bit like folding the clothes after ironing, and not suited to impatient people.

I rang the doorbell, planning to ask whoever answered it if I could look inside.

It didn't occur to me that my aunt would be that person. But she was. She still lived there!

Uncle Phillip was out, at a football match. (It was Saturday afternoon in Manchester.) She was not all that old, actually. About sixty-five, maybe. I had imagined her, all the aunties, as ancient. But all that visiting had taken place when those aunties and uncles were in their thirties, about the age I was myself. She had not changed much. As smart as ever, although in her housekeeping clothes – black jeans, and a loose cream blouse. On her head, a bandana, black and yellow, to protect her hair as she cleaned. She took this off when she saw me and ran a hand through her hair, which was still deep black.

The house was as neat as a pin, and furnished with stuff that surprised me. I would have expected heavy plush English furniture, chintz or thick leather upholstery, mahogany side boards. Instead it was rather understated and elegant. The walls were white. There were some paintings. But also some bits and pieces I recognised – an old fireside chair that had hugged the little fireplace in her parents' flat. A picture of a girl with tears rolling down her cheeks that her mother had loved. Also, a small statue of a saint in a brown and white habit. I remembered that especially, because once I had pointed to it and said, 'The Blessed Virgin?' And my mother had been quite scathing. I should have known that the Blessed Virgin wore only blue and white. 'So who is she?' My mother hesitated, obviously not having a clue. 'Saint Anne,' she said. The Blessed Virgin's mother. She didn't add 'I think' or 'probably'. She wasn't the sort of mother who expressed doubts, to her children. I don't know if it was Saint Anne; I've never seen another plaster statue of her. The Virgin Mary's mother, a bit part in the New Testament.

Auntie Rosaleen gave me tea in a china cup, and chocolate bourbon biscuits which I didn't eat – I rarely ate biscuits then, and certainly never one I didn't like, into which category the bourbons fell. 'Oh, watching your figure!' She, who didn't need to, nibbled one daintily herself as she asked for my parents and my sister and about me and my husband. Did we have kids?

'Two. Two girls.'

'Well, I suppose you've just started.'

'Oh, I don't know.' I mentioned their ages. Four and six. 'I work full time.'

She opened her eyes.

'It used to be all such big families, at home.'

I told her things had changed. What I meant was, we were modern now. The huge families were a thing of the past. Contraception had been legalised in the 1980s. I was on the pill, which I didn't think twice about. I didn't spell it out but she got it.

'Auntie Annabel?'

'She passed away a year ago.'

We had never heard.

'No. You wouldn't.'

Auntie Rosaleen asked me if I would like more tea. I accepted a refill. Tea has no calories to speak of. She offered me a cigarette. I didn't smoke and she lit one herself. The immaculate room seemed to fill with the smell of her cigarette, which was one of those mint-flavoured ones in the green packet.

'Well, you know the story?'

I didn't. Mr and Mrs Surrey had died at some stage, when I was in college – I didn't even remember their funerals. Maybe I'd been away, on one of my summers working in Germany or Denmark or the US, where all the Dublin students went in the summer of their third year. I'd long lost touch with all those aunties and uncles, and my parents had also stopped their round of Dublin social calls. Maybe the television had something to do with this?

The story was that Auntie Annabel got married. This happened soon after her last visit to us. She'd been involved with the fella for years. A married man. 'None of us knew anything about it, of course. Until she came and told us she was married.' Ha! He had got a divorce. He was a doctor, in the hospital where she worked.

'If they thought that would cut any ice back home, they were in for a land.'

Mr Surrey was livid. And Mrs Surrey was terrified. They told Annabel they didn't want to see her again. But finally Mrs Surrey wrote and asked her to come over – she couldn't stand the separation.

Annabel and her husband – Eric – flew over and stayed in a hotel. They had to keep a low profile. Mr Surrey was kept in the dark – he would have killed Eric, if he had met him. 'Well, at least he would have wanted to!' Rosaleen added, explaining that Eric was about twice the size of her father. She was one of those people who tended to overexplain, but I didn't feel impatient, as I usually did when this happened.

'The thing is, dear, they were ashamed. They were eaten up with shame. What would everyone think? The neighbours. Your mother. It was as if she were dirty, as if she was a prostitute, in their eyes.'

Nobody in Ireland would have known he was divorced unless they told them, I pointed out.

'They would have found out. You know what people are like, over there.'

'Everything has changed now. Ireland is different.'

'Do you have divorce?'

She asked archly, with an ironic lift of tone.

No. It was the late 1980s. There had been a referendum but it had been defeated.

'Well then.' She lit another cigarette.

'But it really is different.'

'Well. It doesn't matter. My mother and father have

passed away, God rest them. And so has Annabel.'

'But her husband is alive? Eric?'

I wondered what he made of us. The Irish.

'Oh yes. He's retired. He goes to Scotland. They had a cottage on an island. Barra, I think.'

'It's such a sad story,' I said, just to round things off because it was time for me to go. There was a dinner at the hotel to finish the conference.

I didn't feel sad at all. I felt a bit tired, and … I don't know what. Embarrassed on behalf of my country.

'Remember how your mother said the rosary every night when we were visiting?'

I remembered.

'Does she still do that?'

'She didn't even do it then, when you weren't there.' Only during those visits from England. Look! Holy Catholic Ireland in action.

When Auntie Rosaleen and Phillip and Diana had come to stay with us, we'd all said the rosary every evening after tea. Auntie Rosaleen and Diana would be forced to join in. We knelt on the sitting room floor, leaning against the sofa and armchairs. I imagined I could get a whiff of personal smells if I walked through the gathering of backsides, because most of us slouched into the cushions, as we listened to the soporific mantra, Hail Mary, Holy Mary.

Uncle Phillip always left the room. Perhaps he was asked to? Had my mother said, 'We're going to pray now, Phillip! Off you go.'? I don't recall. Anyway he was expected to leave, and no doubt he wanted to. Unless it was raining, he went out to the garden. There he would stand and smoke a pipe or two, in his solitary Protestant way.

It was always August. The plum tree was heavy with deep leaves. The apples – the buxom green Bramleys, the petite Cox's Orange Pippins – were ripening on the embracing branches of our two trees.

Visby

I had just cycled through the south gate of Visby when my mobile, which was in the bicycle basket, rang. There is a little cobbled square just inside the city walls. I stopped, fished the phone out, and answered. It was Marita, a friend in Ireland, who asked me if I'd heard about Maurice. When somebody from Ireland asks that question on a long-distance call it usually means one thing: the person they name has died. And yes. Maurice was dead. He had drowned in a boating accident. So had his wife and two children. This happened on a fine day in calm waters, on the Irish Sea. They were sailing out beyond Portmarnock. 'It was a glorious day.' Marita paused. There was a moment of silence. 'How tragic,' I said. 'I don't know what to say.'

What I was thinking was, had the boating accident been caused deliberately? Maurice, a colleague of mine and Marita's, exactly my age, was an enthusiastic and experienced sailor.

'I'll let you know about the arrangements,' Marita said, and we ended the conversation.

I sat down on one of the park benches in the middle of the square, under a tree, to collect myself.

It was a beautiful day on Gotland. Mid-June. I had just spent a few hours cycling in the countryside, along the coast at first, and then back by an inland road. The island of Gotland – Visby is the capital – is an exquisite place, especially in summer. On my right, the calm blue Baltic, fringed by little beaches where you could watch the shore birds foraging, where you can forage yourself for ancient fossils. Lilacs and laburnums were abundant in the gardens, and the roadsides bright with blue chicory, camomile daisies and another purple flower that I couldn't identify. Gotland is flat so cycling is easy. I had had an afternoon of perfect pleasure. It had been one of those harmonious interludes when everything coalesces to create a sensation of well-being – the air, the flowers and leaves, the blue bicycle. I'd felt I was floating in the mild sweet air, as lightly and naturally as a bird in flight.

Now, back to earth, with this reminder that life is as precarious as it is precious.

Maurice wasn't a close friend of mine. In fact he wasn't a friend at all really, just an acquaintance, a person I saw around college. I'd never had a coffee with him, or visited his house, or phoned him up to chat – which simple activities are, I suppose, the marks of a friendship, if you need some set of proofs. So I was not personally affected by the news of his death. I could sense that Marita was. I knew she was not closely acquainted with him either, but I realised that she was responding with more emotion than I could honestly feel. I thought it most unfortunate for Maurice that his life was over, and something in me sank or darkened when I allowed myself to suspect that he might have murdered his wife and two children, boys aged ten and eight. Was Maurice one of those men who seem normal and kind at work, but at home metamorphose into a monstrous bully? Street angel, house devil. He wouldn't be the first one. But this was a thought, and insofar as it was an emotion it was anger, not grief. Anger is what I feel when a death is unfair, and the death of a child in an accident is always unfair. I don't believe we feel deep sorrow after any death but one which deprives us of someone who is very close to us, who is an intimate, regular participant in our lives. When people say 'How sad!' about the death of, say, a famous person they never even met, I am taken aback. I wonder if there is something wrong with me. Maybe I'm colder than I like to think. Or maybe when they say, 'How sad!' they simply mean that the fact of death itself is sad. Some might argue with that, even. Death is very sad when it takes away someone you love. Where others are concerned, it's easy to be philosophical about it – mortality is the price we pay for life. If we weren't going to die, would we place much value on life?

I was wondering about this, on the bench in the south square of the perfect old city. There weren't many people about. Saturday evening. The sun was still bright, of course, but the shops were starting to close, people were at home in their houses or hotels, preparing for dinner.

Somebody sat down beside me on the bench. Somebody I knew. A woman I visited twice a week, to practise my Swedish.

I should explain that I was, at this time, staying in a university residence for the month of June. I speak Swedish but there is not much opportunity to practise, at home in Ireland, and there wasn't much opportunity in the residence either. Many of the other residents were foreign, like me, and English was the lingua franca. The Swedes who were there, or in the university, seemed to prefer to speak English. English is a 'killer language', which has sent many tongues to their graves, including Irish, but the Swedes seemed unconcerned about the ultimate fate of their own linguistic heritage, although they conserved stone walls and houses with exquisite care. To cut a long story short, I had to seek out a Swede who would be prepared to let me speak her language for two hours a week. Hulda was happy to oblige. I'd offered to pay for the privilege but she had refused. She was elderly, a retired banker, and pleased enough to do me a favour.

'What a happy coincidence!' Hulda exclaimed. 'I did not notice it was you!'

I murmured something to the effect that I had stopped to take a phone call. Hulda looked at me with an expression of concern. I wondered if I was somehow looking shocked, in spite of everything. I told her that I had had some surprising news, and expanded.

'*Ush*!' That's the expression of dismay (or disapproval) used by Swedes. (Sometimes they say '*Oy oy oy*!') Hulda is in her seventies, at least – naturally I never asked her her age. Her hair is snow-white and clipped short, the style favoured by so many women as they become older. She has large blue eyes, very regular features, and a neat face and body. It is obvious that she was a beauty once, and still is up to a point. 'That's tragic.'

'Yes.' I went on, explaining that Maurice was an acquaintance, not a close friend, and yet …

'And yet that sort of news affects one more deeply than one might expect,' she said. 'You look very pale. Would you like a cup of coffee? Or a drink?'

We went to a nearby cafe – every second house in Visby is

a cafe or restaurant. Sitting in a soft armchair in a corner, I accepted a coffee and a small brandy, a thing I never drink but it seemed appropriate in time of shock, if that's what I was experiencing. Hulda called it an 'avec' and poured hers into her coffee. After a few sips I did likewise. It was much easier to drink that way.

'There have often been drownings in Gotland, especially in the past, but even now,' she said.

And she told me the story of the Eriksons.

Olaf Erikson worked with her at the bank for several years. He joined the staff when he was in his twenties; it was one of his first jobs. A tall thin man, with a hooked nose and big eyes, he was handsome enough but he had a peculiarity: strange ears. They were large and so flabby that they hung down, almost like the ears of an elephant. The reason for this was that they had been frostbitten when he was a boy. One winter not long after the War was extremely cold, and like many people during those years, he was poor and didn't have a proper hat – the expensive thick fur hat with ear flaps that is needed in temperatures of minus thirty. He risked going out in a little cloth cap that didn't cover his ears, with the result that they froze. This minor deformity may have made him self-conscious about his appearance. For whatever reason, he was exceptionally quiet, preferred to work behind the scenes, and never flirted with or even chatted to the young women in the bank, who, according to Hulda, were a lively bunch. He was extremely good with figures and could do a very long tot in seconds, with total accuracy. He had a mind like a computer.

Although he was a man of very few words, he came across as natural, and was scrupulously polite and considerate. If a colleague needed help with anything he was always ready to come to their aid. He was utterly reliable and punctual to a fault, and everyone respected him immensely. And they also actually liked him, even though it wasn't possible to get close to him. He was everyone's acquaintance, nobody's friend.

It came as a great surprise to the others when he married, about three years after he had joined the bank. They wondered how he had even managed to meet a girl, still less to get her to marry him. But the miracle had happened. And she was not any old girl, but a lovely young woman, with thick black hair and dark eyes, who worked in the post office, on the telephone exchange. Her name was Karen and she was not shy or reclusive at all, but quite extrovert and sparkling, according to reports. In Visby everyone knew everyone else, at that time. It wasn't like now, with so many summer houses in the city, inhabited by people who come in June and leave in August, whom you wouldn't really get to know. Karen was not from Visby itself but from a village on the north coast. She was a bit older than Olaf – thirty to his twenty five – and had been in the telephone exchange for two or three years.

Not that he introduced her to Hulda or his workmates. He did not even tell them he was getting married until it was a fait accompli. They had the obligatory marzipan cream cake with their morning coffee the day after they learned of the marriage, and he smiled and accepted the congratulations graciously. At work he continued as usual, doing the accounts in a back office, punctilious to a fault. But anyone could see he was happy. There was a lightness in his movements, the way he carried himself, which had not been evident before. And he whistled sometimes as he walked around the streets. He didn't seem conscious that he was doing this, although he was a very good whistler of snatches of classical music, mainly Mozart.

He and Karen had an apartment in the new part of town that was beginning to expand. Gotland had always been a destination for tourists but it was becoming more and more popular, and rich people from Stockholm and Germany were beginning to buy the little old cottages on the cobbled streets inside the walls, and renovate them. The natives were moving out, some said they were being pushed out, to the modern suburbs. 'Inside the walls', which before had meant nothing much, now came to mean rich and exclusive. And still Visby remained a small town, so even if you couldn't afford a quaint cottage with hollyhocks in the garden you were never far away from them. Olaf, and Karen, who kept her job, walked to work. They were often to be seen strolling around the city, or along by the coast on the walk that stretched from Visby to Snäck, or in the botanical gardens down by the sea. She was always laughing and talking and he was silent – they appeared to complement one another rather neatly.

But nobody was ever invited to their apartment. Their own company seemed all they needed. They listened to music, and spent a lot of time playing chess. They both loved doing crossword puzzles. (The neighbours knew all this, apparently. How they knew, if they never got inside the apartment, wasn't clear to me. I let that go.)

A few years after his marriage Olaf left the bank for a new job, with the army. The Cold War was in full spate and there was then a big military presence on Gotland, which is vulnerable to transgression from the east – the Russians. Olaf, however, was involved with the UN peacekeeping force. He went to Lebanon where he was stationed for four years. Mainly he worked as an interpreter – he had a gift for languages, and for code cracking. Karen remained in

Sweden and continued to work at her job.

Around this time it became known that she had a child, a child who had been born in another relationship, before she married Olaf. Her son was now about twelve years old, and had been adopted or fostered by a family on the mainland. When Olaf was away Karen got in touch with her son and invited him to visit, and then to stay with her for holidays. He came over on the ferry and spent a few nights on the island, but he didn't want to stay. He was happy with his family in Stockholm. His name was Bjorn.

Olaf came home for holidays, and after five years his commission was finished, and he returned to Visby. He got a job with Swedish television, in the accounting department. They continued to live in their old apartment, and life went on as before. Karen had been more sociable when Olaf was abroad – she had been in the habit of going to the movies with a colleague from the post office, and she was a member of a sewing circle which met once a week, in the houses or flats of the various members. All this continued, except that the circle never met in her flat now that Olaf was home. She explained that he had to spend the evenings in peace and quiet and hated to go out, and they accepted that.

At this point I interjected.

There had been cases in Ireland in which a family, or a couple, lived a secluded, almost isolated life, very like that which Hulda was describing, as it seemed to me. But eventually it always emerged that the isolation was enforced by the man, and that he was habitually violent.

No. There was no suspicion of that as far as Olaf was concerned. In the apartment, it would have been difficult, impossible, to conceal physical violence, which is invariably noisy. And everyone could see that Olaf and Karen were a very happy and well-matched couple, although unusual. Besides, Karen was not kept in total isolation. Not only did she continue to work until retirement age, she maintained her friendships with one or two women, and she went to the cinema and the sewing club. And she and Olaf went on their walks at all times of the year. They swam during the summer from the fossil beaches. They had a car and drove around the island.

Did they go on holidays?

Hulda didn't know. But she thought not. And that was unusual – Gotland is a small island. Most residents, at least since the fifties, take a trip to the mainland from time to time. And of course recently people take many trips, on sunshine holidays during the winter, on city breaks all over Europe at other times. Not Olaf and Karen. They never budged from Visby.

They both retired around 1990, he under some slight cloud – there had been some misunderstanding or falling out in the TV station. He didn't get on with the new type of manager, who placed at least as much emphasis on image as on substance, and was careless about details.

From then on, the couple was more reclusive than ever.

When Karen was seventy-five, she fell one night in the flat, and was taken to the local hospital. Her injuries were not serious but she was kept in for a week. Olaf visited her every day; in fact he sat by her bedside for five or six hours daily, reading and doing crossword puzzles, attending to her every need.

But it was clear that Karen was not suffering only from the effect of her fall. She was in a fairly advanced stage of dementia. Her memory was affected, of course, and she was also paranoid – in hospital she shouted at the nurses, and uttered curses that sounded astonishing, emerging from her ladylike mouth. She sometimes shouted and cursed Olaf, who took all this in his stride. He was obviously accustomed to it, and endlessly patient – as he had always been with everything throughout his life.

Karen recovered from her injury and returned home to the flat. She was now visited once a week by a social worker, who reported on progress to the health officials. Olaf was able to care for her. At home, her dementia was less acute or obvious than in the hospital, and the paranoid episodes were much less frequent. She was happy, as she had always been, to be with him.

This went on for another year. Then she had another accident – this time, she left the apartment and was run over by a motorcyclist. She escaped with two broken legs and fractures to her ribs, but she was taken by helicopter to the hospital in Stockholm, since the local hospital couldn't deal with some complication this involved.

I had often seen the helicopter, fluttering noisily up from its landing pad outside the hospital, which was on the edge of the sea just beyond the town. It created a strong wind as it rose up, and the seagulls and ducks went into a tizzy and flew away as soon as they heard the first whirr of the propellers.

Olaf accompanied Karen to Stockholm and found somewhere to stay.

She was there for three weeks. Then she was brought back to Gotland and spent another week in the hospital on the island.

At the end of this stay the doctor had a chat with Olaf, and suggested that Karen should move into a home. Her dementia was much worse now, and she was endangering her own life and possibly his. Olaf pointed out, in his quiet, rational, and articulate way, that Karen would hate a home. She hated being in hospital, and that is why her dementia increased and seemed much worse when she was under the care of the medics. He felt if he had some assistance – a daily visit from a nurse, for instance – he would be well able to look after her at home, at least for the time being.

Reluctantly the doctors agreed to his suggestion. Indeed it suited government policy, which was to keep everyone at home for as long as possible, even very old people living alone, some of whom would, if given a choice, have preferred to live in an institution. There was a financial reason for the strategy, although it was always expressed as a policy which was motivated by the best intentions for the patient's, or old person's, well-being. Everyone wants to stay at home until the end, is how they expressed it. Old people did not express this view, and were not asked for their opinion. It had become an accepted 'fact'. (Hulda was quite exercised by this aspect of public policy. I realised she was getting worried about her own future; she lived alone. Her husband had died years earlier and she had some stepchildren, who never visited for some reason. I never thought of her as particularly old, since she was fit and youthful.)

Karen went home again to the flat outside the walls.

Hulda ordered a second brandy, and I took a glass of wine. I don't like brandy and I had almost forgotten why I was here in the first place. The little bistro was getting busier as people came in for their evening meal. The waitress was lighting candles on all the tables. Even though the sun would not go down until eleven or eleven thirty, this cafe, like a lot of the houses in Visby, was rather dark, with narrow penitential windows and low ceilings.

The day before Karen was discharged from hospital,

Olaf went to a builders' supplier and bought a quantity of lead. The shop assistant remembered him and had wondered why he wanted the lead but didn't ask. Olaf wasn't the type to offer an explanation. He carried twenty kilos of lead home, left it in the kitchen, and then walked through the town down to the harbour. At the ticket office he bought one ticket for the ferry to Finland for the following day. The ticket officer asked if he wanted a standard cabin or a luxury cabin and he decided on the latter. She ascertained that it was a ticket for one, since the cabins were designed for two, and he assured her he needed just one return ticket to Helsinki, which he called Helsingfors, like most Swedes of his generation.

Karen came home from hospital in a taxi the following morning, a Friday morning. Olaf gave her a *fika*, a cup of coffee and a cinnamon bun, and had the same himself. They sat at the small coffee table by the window, where they had always sat when doing the crossword, which Karen had been unable to manage for four years now. Soon after drinking the coffee, Karen fell asleep – it had contained several crushed sleeping tablets. Olaf then carried her to her bed in one of the rooms adjoining the big living room, and smothered her with a pillow.

A few hours later, in the late afternoon, he took a small suitcase, which was very heavy, and made his way to the harbour, where he boarded the ship for Finland. He went immediately to his stateroom, a large luxurious apartment with a balcony. That is the last anyone saw of him.

News of Karen's murder became public that night. Bjorn, her son, was the one who found her. Olaf had contacted him and asked him to come over to visit his mother.

Olaf had travelled under his own identity, and it took very little time to discover that he had boarded the ship.

The captain and chief engineer went to his cabin, but it was quite empty. The bed had not been slept in and nothing was disturbed. His small black suitcase was neatly placed on the suitcase stand. It too was empty.

'So he was one of those house devils,' I said, sipping the last of my wine. 'A control freak.'

I tried to say this in Swedish. I may have selected the words clumsily, but Hulda understood. She had the endless patience of the good pedagogue, and she would have died rather than ask me to speak English.

No, she didn't think so. Olaf and Karen were more like a Romeo and Juliet. That's what she thought, and that's what everyone who knew them – or knew who they were, their acquaintances – believed. They were so much in love that they could not bear to live apart. It was the only sensible solution to the problem. Karen would have been taken from him, to a home for demented old people. The thought of life without her was intolerable to him.

'The only person who believed he was a bully was the son, Bjorn. But then, he was one of the few people who had never liked Olaf. I suppose he never forgave him for marrying his mother,' Hulda said, thoughtfully. 'They don't, you know.'

Nadia's Cake

A rooster is crowing. The screech spouts up into the hot air and spreads over the red rooftops like the cry of a spirit from another world – a healthy supernatural being: this voice is loud and triumphant, as well as shrill. Two old men drinking beer at a plastic table outside a ramshackle shop pay no attention at all. They could be deaf. In silence they sit, whiling away the day, on the lookout for something new with eyes that expect disappointment. But today there is a new thing. Jen, the stranger who has just come to town. They don masks of inscrutability, and take every inch of her in, as she walks over the cobbles in her shorts and thick sandals, as she listens to the rooster's scream. To her it's as exotic and delightful as the soft sounds of the language of the village, all shushes and zhuzhes, like the push and slush of the tide on a shingle beach … or the plash of a waterfall in a mountain pool, more appropriate a simile in this inland valley, where she's the exotic one, as surprising and welcome as an elephant or a giraffe.

The houses on the street are like farmhouses, but all

huddled close to one another as if they are engaged in constant gossip. They are silent, though. A few are holiday houses, with pretty terraces, empty now on Tuesday, waiting for the weekend. A few are inhabited, by old people, and they nestle in gardens of flowers and fruit and vegetables, with hens running about. Most of the houses look as if they have been dead for a long, long time.

'Where is everyone?' she asks Nevena, the woman she will stay with, the owner of the 'guest house' – a guest house with one guest and no room for more either. Rose Cottage, it is called. Charming guest house in the picturesque and historic village of Helansi.

'In the city.' Nevena is chunky, her body wrapped snugly in a dark overall, her white hair cropped. She could be seventy. Or eighty. Or ninety. As well as the 'guest house' she runs a shop and a cafe, and keeps chickens, two goats, a garden where tomatoes, cabbages, onions, herbs and roses grow. Also raspberries and peaches and watermelons. 'Or abroad.'

Jen knows. Communism. Corruption. Emigration. But you have to make conversation. Plus, there is a strict limit to the things she can say, or ask. Not for reasons of tact or law. Purely linguistic. She can say very little in Nevena's language. I get up. I dress myself. I eat breakfast.

She has never met anybody who would be interested in the details of her morning routine, although maybe Nevena is an exception. It's hard to create an opening though. Oh yes, I wake up at seven every morning. Really? And what do you do then? I wash myself and brush my teeth.

Nevena talks, not seeming to care that Jen doesn't understand most of what she is saying, and brings a meal on a tray. Tomatoes and cucumbers, a stew of sausages and garlic and beans. Red wine. Raspberries and yoghurt.

Food is a language everyone can understand.

Jen eats at a wooden table on the edge of the garden. Bees hum and there is a lovely smell, a mixture of roses and garlic and thyme. The mountains are not far away, two thousand metres high, covered in forests. In them wild boar roam, bears, and on the rocks in the hot sun lie small snakes with horns on their heads. Their venom is deadly and can kill you in an hour if you don't get the antidote – available in the city, four hours from here. Don't sit on a rock or a stone, Nevena says. Sit on the chair.

Nobody comes here. Nobody knows the village of Helansi exists, apart from those who live here or were born here, or the much larger group whose forebears were born here. It's one of the thousands of villages in the country whose main export has been human beings for the past two hundred years or so.

So how did Jen end up in this place, on a month-long stay? (She calls it a holiday, to people back home.)

By complete accident is the truth of the matter. But, since people prefer to believe that there is a pattern to life she has an alternative answer that she trots out: 'I saw the village when I was on a bus tour of the country a year ago and I fell in love with it.'

Sometimes she substitutes 'I felt completely at home there' or 'I felt I belonged there' for 'I fell in love'. Depending on the audience.

Such rubbish.

You could maybe 'fall in love' with it if you were susceptible to appearances and could ignore the constant harping about how hopeless the country is, how its economy is a disaster and its government corrupt, the gypsies a menace and everything going to hell. You could ignore that and listen to the cheerful clucking of the chickens, the lazy bark of a dog, the hum of summer in the raspberry patches. You could close your ears to the grumbles about crime, corruption and emigration, and just give yourself up to the smell of the roses and the view of a million sunflowers. (Can a country that produces roses and sunflowers as a cash crop be all that bad?) You could ignore your misgivings and feel with pleasure the huge rough cobblestones under your feet, so thick and rough that even your toes know they've been there since the Middle Ages. Like the toy-box church, almost buried in the earth, with the blue and gold and dark red icons inside, and the thin candles spouting from sandy brass stands like blades of scutch grass on the beach.

But how on earth would anyone from Ireland – from Dublin – feel at home here? The temperature thirty-five degrees in summer and minus ten in winter, the language as foreign as Chinese, even the alphabet unintelligible. People veering between overwhelmingly generous (the ones who know you) and icily surly (at bus stations and in some official places). And nobody speaking English, or even French or German ... they look to the rising sun, here, or used to when the denizens of Helansi were at the language-learning stage of life. Their Russian is fine. They can deal with Turkish, and if you happen to be Greek you'll probably get by.

She didn't fall in love, she didn't feel at home, there was no grand design.

If there was any inspiration it was a TV programme.

You must never admit that, to anyone. (A book is okay. A history or even a novel. Best of all a poem or a poet. But she has only read one novel by an author from here and can't name a single poet.)

The TV programme was not about Helansi, or the land

it is in. (All the programmes she has ever seen about this country on TV – mostly on the BBC – focus on its dark side. Lager louts doing unspeakable things at the seaside. The mafia, corruption. If you saw those programmes you'd be scared to set foot in the place.) The programme wasn't a travel show at all, but a counselling session called *How to be Happy*, and was presented by a famous popular psychotherapist. 40 per cent of your happiness is under your own control, she said. 50 per cent is due to inherited genes, and the rest to circumstances. A measly 10 per cent.

When Jen saw this programme the 10 per cent – life circumstances – were at rock bottom. And they were circumstances she could do absolutely nothing about. Except … 'Set a goal,' said the woman on the programme, a rather motherly person with a cheerful face.

Work, in other words.

She opened the internet and looked up language courses. Registered for the first one she found, which began with the letter B. The language B is the language of Helansi.

By curious accident, it is taught as a night class in a Dublin university, a city where otherwise only the most ordinary languages, like French and German, are offered by the universities, due to lack of funding.

She had studied it for two semesters, but she could still only say 'How are you?' And 'I wake up at seven o'clock'. So she came to a village in the mountains where she would have no choice but to listen and learn and speak.

Thank you.

Excuse me.

I'd like a glass of water.

More wine please.

At first she cannot understand Nevena – or, needless to say, anyone else in the village – when Nevena utters simple sentences. But after two days she's getting better.

When you are in a village with no internet, where you can't understand the TV – they all watch a lot of TV; Nevena says she would be dead without it – with no car, no job, no colleagues, time expands. The day is long and the part of night before sleep even longer.

At home, life is full of distractions. Or perhaps the distractions are what constitute life? Going to work. Meeting friends and relations, going to movies or plays or openings, going on hikes. Hoovering, cutting the grass.

Here, everybody works, Nevena says. Jen doesn't ask what those old guys sitting outside the cafe for half the day actually work at. Something. Or maybe their wives work. Nobody can retire because most of their pensions went out the window with communism. Nevena does the hoovering, the cooking, the garden, in between serving in her shop and cafe. She never stops working from morning to night – if she watches TV, it must be in the winter, when there are no vegetables to weed or goats to milk or guests to feed.

Jen has to quickly develop a routine. She reads in the language for the first two hours of the day – laborious dictionary work; it takes an hour to read a page, at least, looking up every second word. When she reaches a sentence that she can read without the dictionary she whoops with delight. (The psychologist was right: any goal will make you happy, at least for a while, when you feel you're making progress towards it.) Then she walks for two hours in the mountains, avoiding rocks and snakes, boars and bears. Then it is lunchtime. Conversation with Nevena – getting longer, as time goes on. They both nap for an hour in the hottest part of the day.

There is still a lot of time to get through.

After naptime, she takes to sitting outside the cafe with the old men.

They are delighted, of course. Jen is several decades younger than they are, and her foreign look – pale skin, blue eyes – makes her interesting, even though she's ugly by comparison with the women of this country. At least the younger ones anyway, who are lithe, olive-skinned, with eyes shaped like dark almonds and flowing black hair. She's so weird by comparison with them that it doesn't matter. She's in another category altogether.

'*An rud is annamh is iontach*,' says Dimitar. One of them.

He says it in his own language but Jen recognises the proverb from hers.

That's when she finds, by accident, a new thing to do.

She can record on her phone.

Mobile phones can do almost anything these days.

She sits outside the cafe. The word is prettier than the fact. The cafe is a shop with a tin roof, selling cigarettes, cans of beans, sliced bread. Newspapers. Also various kinds of alcohol, to take away or drink on the premises, at a plastic table on the shop floor or outside on the broken footpath. That's where she sits, from after nap till dinner at seven. She collects proverbs.

It's her second week.

She sits with the two men.

They know ten proverbs, they say. They underestimate themselves. By the end of the week, they have told her two hundred. They sit under the shelter of the porch, and say them, sometimes explaining the proverb with a little anecdote.

Jen doesn't understand most of what is being said. She nods and smiles. They know she doesn't always get it but they go on anyway.

When it's time to go home for dinner, she thanks them and says goodbye and see you tomorrow.

After dinner she listens back. She transcribes what she can. Sooner than you'd think, it's time for bed.

The third week, they start telling stories. It's easier to understand proverbs than stories. But she pretends, she nods, she says I understand. They don't believe her but they're not entirely sure. And anyway they don't care whether she understands or not, listens or not. They like talking; they're great storytellers. After sitting outside the cafe for years not talking it's fantastic to have an audience, even an audience that doesn't understand what you're saying. She's enthusiastic. What more does a performer want?

She listens back after dinner. She engages Nevena for help. And how can Nevena help? With gestures. With much waving of hands, and pointing, and miming, as in a game of charades.

Some of the stories are about ghosts and some are about vampires and some are about the Ottomans and some are about stepmothers and bears and wolves and the gypsies. All dangerous characters, villains, whom the protagonist – an ordinary girl or boy or man or woman – vanquishes. Or not. These dangerous characters are to some extent interchangeable. Dimitar tells a story about a devil, and Nikolaj more or less the same story about a bear. A wild boar, a vampire, a gypsy? Take your pick.

Jen is shocked by the attitude of her old men, her friends, her storytellers, towards the gypsies, their neighbours. (She doesn't mind that they are prejudiced against bears and boars, also their neighbours, up in the old mountain; she shares their sentiments.) The prejudice against travellers in

Ireland is as nothing compared to this. She refrains from criticism. Who is she to ride a middle-class Irish high horse through a Balkan village?

One day at the start of the third week, Jen gets the bus to town.

Nevena disapproves of the bus. Of Jen getting the bus. It's not exactly clear why. It doesn't come on time. We don't know when it will come. Nevena thinks Jen should get a taxi. Thirty kilometres to town. Jen says, as best she can, that she likes travelling by bus. She likes seeing the other people, the ordinary people, on the bus and she gets a better view of the landscape than she would from a taxi.

The gypsies get the bus. They hang around the bus stop. That's what Nevena says. That's what she has against it.

For heaven's sake.

Jen gets the bus.

And of course nobody robs her or rapes her or otherwise interferes with her. There are, on the bus, six or seven other passengers, of various ages. Some gypsies, some not. Jen can't tell the difference. The bus stops at various villages and picks up more people. Mostly they are going to work, and some are going to shop in town. She is able to ask the driver when there will be a return bus and he gives exact times. Half past one. Five o'clock.

The town consists of two or three streets and a plaza, and then a sprawl of houses, apartment blocks. And the gypsy village, a shanty town on the outskirts. A few carts are being driven along the small road into the village, pulled by skinny horses that run at high speed. The carts are beautiful and simple, made of unpainted wood. A driver and a few passengers can fit in one, and stuff. Things they have bought at the market.

Jen walks around the town, to get an overview, to

see what it has to offer. Which is several small shops – a bakery, grocery shops, a few small drapers, chemists, tobacconists. There is a small supermarket and a shop selling toys and hardware. A library, a folklore museum, a bank. In the middle of the big square a fountain plays; the sparkling silver water creates a sense of coolness, although in fact it is hotter here in the town, small as it is, than in the village.

She buys what she needs – paper, copy books, new biros – and tries to enquire at the library if it's possible to print out something from her USB stick. It is. But they can't do more than six pages. Jen has about a hundred. She will be allowed to leave them and collect them in a few days. Okay.

Then she has to find a new USB stick. This takes a while. The toyshop, it turns out, is the place that has such things, jumbled up with plastic *Frozen* dolls and soft teddy bears.

When all this business is finished she has two hours left before the bus comes. Coffee outside the surprisingly modern, stylish cafe, a look at the folklore museum – folk costumes from the region, mummers' masks, kitchen implements.

She's back in the village at 2 p.m. Nevena is relieved to see her.

'Do you go to town yourself?'

Nevena shakes her head. 'Not often. I get everything I need here.'

A delivery van brings the supplies for the shop, limited as they are. And, Nevena says, her daughter comes up sometimes. She lives in the town.

This opens the door to a conversation they have not had, about families. Nevena volunteers plenty of information, about 30 per cent of which Jen understands. One of her daughters lives in the town – she is married with two children, both of whom have emigrated to London, where they work in shops. They have university degrees but they work like me, she says, except I own my own shop and they work in Lidl. Stacking shelves. On the checkout if they're in luck. She has a second daughter who lives in the capital city and comes to see her on Christmas Day, in the morning, then drives back again. Unless the snow is too heavy.

And you? Nevena would like some information in return.

Jen shakes her head. 'I'm not married,' she says. 'No children.'

She has told Nevena about her job. She's a teacher. She can't say she's on a career break – too complicated at more than one level. Nevena assumes she's on her summer holidays. Teachers, everyone knows, like to spend their summer holidays doing strange things, like learning something new. Learning is a rest from all that teaching.

Ah! says Nevena, also shaking her head. She pours a glass of wine for Jen, from the bottle on the windowsill, even though they don't drink wine at lunchtime, usually.

A few days later Jen gets the bus again. This time she asks to be let off at the railway station, which is on the edge of the town, near the gypsy settlement. She plans to walk past that, take photographs, and walk the rest of the way into the centre where she'll pick up her printouts from the library.

The bus driver stops and lets her out. Some of the passengers stare at her, maybe disapprovingly. She still finds it hard to interpret their expressions. Mostly their faces seem completely blank and inscrutable. These are people who can keep secrets.

The railway station has the ramshackle look many public buildings here have – peeling paint, weeds growing through the cracks in the concrete. There is not much sign of life – a local train passes a few times a day, the train to Istanbul once, during the night, and it doesn't stop here. There's nobody about on the road, either, as she begins her walk. Most of the fields are full of sunflowers; in a few the crop is Indian corn, higher than Jen's head. She takes photos, she listens to the birdsong, sees what she thinks is an eagle, and three white owls asleep on the top of a tall tree.

It's still early, and the sun is not scorching, but pleasant on her bare arms, bare legs. She feels a lightening in her body that she has not felt for years – here comes one of those moments of glad grace, that arrive unannounced, like the visit of an angel, that you can never plan for, anticipate, that can last for a minute or an hour or a day, but will always go, a mood that is like the wind or a white cloud in the sky, over which she absolutely no control. One of the white clouds has not visited her for three years.

And here it is now, on this little road through the sunflower fields.

She hears a cart rumbling behind her, and the fast clip clop, a sound so unfamiliar that she just realises it's a horse trotting a second before something happens to her head.

Next.

She is in a dim room. It is not unlike the rooms she knows in the village – a big plasma TV, a table covered with oilcloth, an iron range. But there's some difference, some hint of something – poorer, or shabbier, or maybe just other. A woman is cooking something at the range and two men are hovering over Jen.

The gypsies have darker skin than the other people. Just a little bit darker, and otherwise their features are the same. The men, though, have an expression in their eyes that is a mixture of ferocity and hopelessness.

Jen wonders what will happen now … she wonders as if 'she' were a third party. She feels, for now, curiosity, rather than fear.

One of the men, who is older – they are father and son, she surmises – says something.

She doesn't understand. The gypsies speak two languages – the language of the land, with a different accent, and another language. She wouldn't understand anyway. But she knows this guy is speaking the other language deliberately, to make sure she can't understand.

She does not have a headache. Aren't you supposed to, after a bang on the head that knocks you out?

The woman comes and gives her water, in a plastic cup. Jen wonders if she should drink it – maybe it's poisoned? But she decides it's better to take the risk, rather than offend them by refusing. And as soon as she sees the water she becomes aware of an enormous thirst. She swallows it quickly and gives back the cup, and the woman fills it again. This happens three times.

Jen is not sick, and she is still alive. It tasted just like ordinary water. But now her head begins to ache.

The young man comes over to her and grins, not in a very friendly way. He has enormous teeth. Graveyard teeth. He pulls her credit card out of his pocket and shows it to her. So they want her to take out money and give it to them.

She shakes her head. She has remembered, just in time,

that in this country you shake your head when you mean yes, and give a sort of a funny little half-nod when you mean no.

She is thinking very clearly. How will they manage this? The logistics. Get her to the ATM – it's outside the bank beside the toy shop. Wait and get the money. How will they manage all this, without being observed by the people shopping – all of them suspicious? And the ATM is just across the street from the police station. She'll break free. She'll get away from them as soon as she gets there.

He – the young one, he is wearing a blue checked shirt, rather fresh and nice-looking – hands her a piece of paper and a biro. So. She won't be going to the ATM. She writes down her PIN number. The young man shakes his head – thanks – and leaves. She fancies she hears the horse, clip clop, off to town. How many miles to Dublin town? she finds the song going through her head. Three score and ten, sir.

Her feet are tied with a rope. Her current account, the one she withdraws money from, contains ten thousand euro. He can take out four hundred, max, in one day. Or maybe five hundred. But he can find out how much is in it, easily, by pressing the check balance button.

Why did she leave all that money in the current account?

She knows why. She didn't know how much she would need, over here, how long she would stay. So she transferred her savings to the account attached to her card.

How many days till all the money is gone? A few hundred a day … How many miles to Dublin town?

Nevena baked stuffed peppers for the late lunch, with, as always, tomato and cucumber salad. She had chicken soup herself at twelve, to keep the wolf from the door. When the bus came back to the village at two without Jen on board she was suspicious and phoned the police – the nearest station in the town. They told her to wait for the evening bus. Jen had most probably decided to stay in town for the afternoon. Most people come back after a day or two. They always say that.

At seven Nevena was back on the phone, complaining. Something had happened to Jen. She knew it.

'Most people come back in a few days,' they said again.

Next morning Nevena took the bus herself. She asked the driver about Jen. He remembered her. So did everyone on the bus. She got off at the railway station. Did she get a train? Much nodding of heads. No, there was no train, then, and they saw her walking along the road taking photographs. They agreed that that the gypsies had probably got her. What else would you expect? She had the camera and money and credit cards. One woman expressed the view that Jen was already dead. They'll kill her for her credit card, mobile phone. The camera looked expensive.

Nevena was inclined to agree. It would be easy to dispose of Jen. They'd dump her in the lake, dead (or alive). They'd take her up the mountain and bury her in the forest, in a shallow grave where animals could finish her off. Who would ask about her? She seemed to have no friends or relatives. She wasn't married (she said, although Nevena didn't believe her; Jen looked like a married woman – Nevena could tell).

Nevena got off at the police station, just across from the ATM. She handed the police officer an envelope containing fifty euro, and reported Jen missing again. Her suggestion was that they search the gypsy village.

No. They didn't like going into the gypsy settlement because they got a bad reception there – a pelting with eggs and tomatoes, at best. Would they risk their lives for an Irish woman who was – in the policeman's opinion, now expressed – in the city, living in a luxury hotel, shopping and eating in summer cafes? It was no surprise to him that Jen was bored with life in Helansi. Everyone was bored with life in Helansi. There was nothing as boring as the deserted villages of this country. That's why all the young people left. Only those who had no choice stayed there.

The mother has a name. Nadia.

Although her son looks to be about twenty, Jen sees that Nadia is not much more than thirty. The son must be younger than he looks. Fifteen or sixteen. The gypsies, it is said, tend to skip school, although like everyone else they are supposed to go until they are sixteen. They grow up fast. They have to, to survive.

Nadia gives Jen tea, and thick vegetable soup, when the men go out. Initially the plan seemed to be that one man would always be at home to keep watch on the prisoner. But after the first day they both go out. Keeping guard isn't much fun, obviously. Jen's feet are tied, they trust Nadia to guard her – she would not dare to do anything else. They seem to be called Ivan. Both of them.

But she gives her the soup, and tea made with herbs. Once, she gives her pastry stuffed with cheese. Nadia goes outside and comes back with peppers and tomatoes and onions and mint. She must have a little garden outside the shack, just like Nevena. She is, Jen concludes, pretty much like the people in the village.

You're not doing anthropological studies now, thinks

Jen. Her headache is gone. And her camera. He has taken it away, he has probably sold it, although you'd wonder where, in the little town. Who'd want it? They have contacts, maybe, with people in the city?

You could not say Nadia is friendly. She has that inscrutable expression Jen is now familiar with. The look she calls 'communist'. (Everything you cannot quite understand is called 'communist' – shrug – in this country, especially everything negative.) But she is kind. She offers the soup and tea, and water from time to time. (The soup is excellent.) Sometimes, from her perch near the stove or the table, she glances over at Jen, with a question in her eye. Do you need anything?

Jen knows how to ask for the toilet and Nadia can understand her accent. Going to the toilet isn't easy. It involves untying the ropes, which turned out to be very difficult. (Apparently the Ivans have not considered the possibility that the toilet issue would arise. She must be their first kidnappee then? You'd imagine anyone with experience of keeping prisoners would have a plan – or a potty.)

No. Untie the ropes. Then tie them again, around Jen's waist! Then out the back of the shack. That's it. There is a little tin hut with a chemical toilet. Nadia insists that the door be left ajar. Jen is constipated. Naturally. Minutes pass. She is able to look around. There's the garden. There are raspberries, and the peppers and onions and tomatoes and cucumbers. A peach tree. The garden is pretty, with flowers and fruit, but temporary-looking – even though the gypsies are not nomads, they have been here, probably in this very place or nearby, for about three hundred years. But the culture is 'we're ready to move on'. Here is no fixed abode. (Not their fault.)

Thinking anthropological thoughts is more relaxing

than thinking about what fate has in store for her. She signals to Nadia that she's ready, although sitting here in the latrine is at least out of doors and more interesting than the house.

Can I wash my hands?

She can say all these things now, fluently, without difficulty. Being kidnapped has done wonders for her knowledge of the language.

There is a bucket and basin on an old table ... even soap. Lovely soap with the strong rose scent all the soap and cream and stuff has here – soap made from rose oil. A bathroom practically, in the open. Must be cold in winter out here ... maybe they bring in the bucket and basin and bar of soap.

The sun is high. She can see through gaps in houses a field of sunflowers. Also a building she thinks she recognises – a derelict factory, where the gypsies used to have jobs during communism. After the change, the factories closed, nothing came to replace them.

She knows where she is. Not all that far from Nevena and the mountain village.

Nadia puts her back on the cushion and ties her up again, not quite as well as the Ivans do it. Jen wonders, as she feels the looseness of the knot, if she can escape at some stage. Loosen the rope gradually, the way captive criminal detectives do so easily in TV dramas. Then make a run for it. But there are many houses in the settlement and a lot of nasty-looking dogs. Even if she succeeded in doing that thing with the rope, she probably wouldn't get very far.

Another bowl of soup, this time with a piece of bread. Another night on the floor with Ivan the Younger sleeping in a sleeping bag in front of the door, his knife out beside him, at the ready. It gleams in the dark. If she could get out of the ropes, she could, if she were very quick and quiet, grab the knife while he slept, leap over him like a silent cunning fox and run.

But she can't get out of the rope even though she has watched people doing it on TV hundreds of times. Wriggle, wriggle, wriggle desperately, and finally it gives. No. And she doesn't know how to stab people. She's not very good at carving meat, even. Her father used to carve the roast beef for Sunday dinner – the only culinary activity he ever engaged in. Traditionally, men do the carving at the table, and it is mainly men who do the stabbing. (She can allow her thoughts to wander; there's plenty of time to think, when you're tied up all day long.) You need that strength they have – men, that is – that can tie ropes tightly, and remove nuts from wheels ... things she can never do herself, although she looks strong enough.

Breakfast is yoghurt and a slice of red watermelon. Ivan the Younger gives her a sceptical look as she eats it and grits his big teeth. Possibly thinking it's a waste of good food, giving it to her. He'll be off to the ATM as soon as he's finished his own enormous bowl of yoghurt, and what looks like a loaf of bread. The standard of the meals is getting higher in the house. That'll be thanks to the subvention from her bank account. The third day – he's already taken out 1500, and here that's worth twice as much as at home. He'll buy himself something today when he hits the two thousand mark, she'd bet her bottom dollar. What? New shoes, maybe? He'd like shiny pointy leather boots, teddy-boy boots. Or maybe a cool black leather jacket?

Of course he might buy a gun.

She doesn't know where she got that idea. It just popped into her head. But it stops her in her spooning of another dollop of yoghurt (she likes this yoghurt, so healthy and fresh) from bowl to mouth. As soon as the thought strikes her, she knows she's right. That's exactly what he'll buy. He'll know where to get one. It's the investment his career as a criminal needs. Armed with a gun, instead of that stupid-looking carving knife, there'll be no stopping Ivan the Younger. The world will be his oyster then – he'll be able to hold up banks, rob post offices, frighten the daylights out of girls and women and grab their purses. Take the cash registers from the little grocery shops, sweet shops, vegetable shops that are everywhere, usually run by little old ladies. Easy prey. With a gun in his pocket he could do the rounds in his horse and cart, cleaning up all before him. Ivan the Kid, scourge of the Wild East.

He smiles at her, as if reading her thoughts. As he passes he gives her a not unfriendly kick in the leg. Time to go to the bank, he says winking.

Best of luck, she says.

That makes him scowl. But he doesn't kick her.

Nadia doesn't want to bring her to the bathroom.

Why? Because she knows Ivan is going to shoot her as soon as he gets back from the bank with his new gun? Why waste time bothering about the toilet? Soon Jen will be in the vegetable patch, fertilising it (as if it needed more). She'll be pushing up the sunflowers.

No. It's just that Nadia is extra busy today. She was up earlier than usual, and out to the garden at the crack of dawn, picking things, collecting the eggs. Now she's baking something. Bread? There's sugar, a slab of butter, eggs, on the table. A jug of something that looks like cream.

Nadia is baking a cake.

Visitors?

Jen, by now as quick to jump to ethnic stereotyping as anyone who has been raised in that culture, supposed the extended family lived together, in this village, although nobody apart from the immediate family has come into the house since she arrived. But maybe they have relatives somewhere else? Just like non-gypsies. What will they do with her when the visitors come?

Maybe the visitors are coming for her? To take her away to the mountains? Goodness knows what they'd do with her if they got her into the forest. Toss her to a brown bear, just for the fun of it? Abandon her in the woods to take her chances, like a child in a fairy tale. (They're the lucky ones, who get abandoned. Some person or animal always comes along to rescue them.)

It is in the oven. The sweet smell of baking cake fills the room, imbues it with a warm welcoming mood.

I have to go, says Jen. She cannot say 'if I don't I won't be responsible for the consequences.' So she says again, I have to go, I have to go.

Nadia sighs and releases her, not bothering to tether her at the waist.

But she does follow Jen out to the yard. Jen crouches down on the smelly toilet, concentrating on the raspberries outside.

Hurry up! Nadia says. Unusual for her to say anything.

I'm doing it as fast as I can, Jen says. Sorry!

The stink has competition now. A smell from the house. The baking cake.

Burning.

Oh God!

Nadia dashes into the kitchen. But not before she has said one last word to Jen.

'Бягай!'

Jen understands the word, all right. She'd get it even if she didn't know it, from Nadia's tone.

She pulls up her pants and runs off without stopping to wash her hands. There are no fences here so she doesn't have to scale one. She just runs and runs, through the sprawl of houses, the shanty town. People look at her, dogs look at her, dogs bark, but nobody stops her gallop. They mustn't know about her, mustn't know that the Ivans have a prisoner in their house, and a debit card that will make their fortune.

She's through the looking glass again. She's back in the garden, drinking coffee and eating the pastry stuffed with cheese that Nevena offers for breakfast as a weekend treat – the pastry Nadia also offered, once.

She's thinking, maybe I will go back to Dublin. The Irish Travellers are nice people, mostly. She's never heard that they kidnap people. They just come to her house and try to persuade her to get new gutters and fascia boards, or to tar the driveway. Sometimes they want to cut Jen's hedge. She often lets them do that. But even when she refuses to indulge their passionate desire to pour tar on the driveway they don't kidnap her or tie her up.

But it's not warm and sunny. There's not so much fresh fruit and vegetables, and the mountains are not as high and wild. And it's lonely. Three years ago, her baby, aged one, died of meningitis. That's her past story. Jen isn't a criminal on the run. She hasn't killed anyone, she doesn't carry some unspeakable burden of guilt.

Just ordinary sadness, which, it is possible, the passage of time will lighten, although probably not cure.

Dublin is a sad city, for her. At the moment. It's a sad place. All she wants is a new country, a new language, new food. New people, new stories. She wants all this newness – which is as old as the hills – to enclose her, nourish her, remake her. She feels, still, she can renew herself in a completely new place. She feels this, though she doesn't really believe it. It is a faint hope, like the hope the old men in the village have that something new might happen today, as they walk down the village street. A visitor. Some good news. Some small everyday miracle.

Nevena says, you should go somewhere else. You could go to the city. Or the sea.

The city, Nevena thinks, is full of people who look more or less like Jen. As is the coast. The Black Sea.

I like it here, says Jen. Actually she says, I love it here, because it is easier to say the words for 'I love' than for 'I like', which has some tricky syntax. When she says it, though, she realises it's true. She loves it here.

She decides to stay and go on collecting stories from the old guys. She will stay until the end of September, when the weather will change and leaves will fall. Then she can consider where to go next, on her journey.

She wonders what happened to Nadia's cake. Who ate it? What did it taste like?

Baltic Amber

The medium-size suitcase – the blue one – is packed. Now Linda is putting the finishing touches to her face before heading off to the airport. Of course there will be time to brush up a bit at the other end, before she gets to passport control, but the main things have to be seen to now. Hair washed and puffed out to make it look a bit thicker; face smoothed with foundation, eyebrows coloured in with that eyebrow kit she got recently. A dot of concealer over the warty thing on her temple. (It's a geriatric spot, her brother told her. 'Sorry, sis!' Linda's dermatologist says it's something else. A blood vessel. 'I don't touch them,' she said. The dermatologist speedily and painlessly lasers off rather harmless-looking freckly sunspots, but this thing, which looks like a big slimy black beetle, is here to stay.)

She has found a dress that is comfortable enough to travel in and is reasonably flattering. It's black, which can't be helped, although since now it's spring she'd like to wear a lighter colour. Pale lemon, mint green. The summery colours she owns are lightweight (also, packed). It's cold for the time of year. There was a shower of sleet just after she woke up. She can lift the blackness with a necklace, and earrings.

But when she roots around on the untidy dressing table, among the pots of face cream, the hairbrushes and various little boxes, she can't find any.

Well, actually she can find quite a few – a dozen at least – but no two that match.

Even the amber ones, which she has managed to keep for almost five years, and had planned to wear today, have vanished.

In her life, Linda has lost a hundred-odd earrings. More. Odd is the right word. Usually one earring goes missing, its comrade remaining to languish alone in a jewellery box or drawer until such a time as she throws it out – just like leftover dinner in the fridge. Sometimes, in a fit of creativity, she wears just one earring, or two odd (but rather similar) ones – two pearls, say, one a bit bigger than the other. Why do the two earrings have to be exactly the same? It's just tradition, like so much that dictates what we wear and how we wear it. The rings on her fingers – five, to her surprise, when she counts – are all different, after all. Nobody expects anything else. On the contrary.

Of course, her two ears are identical, at least to the naked eye. Whereas the five fingers on each hand are different from one another. Still, most of the finger rings are on the two ring fingers. Also a matter of tradition. There is really no good reason not to wear rings on any of the other four fingers, never mind the thumb. Although if you look closely at your thumb, you'll also wonder why it never gets a ring.

Usually after about half an hour of wearing two odd

earrings Linda pulls off both of them. They make her feel uncomfortable. They make her feel, and probably look, odd. In the sense of eccentric, possibly forgetful, possibly crazy.

Earrings are symbolic, if you know the language of earrings. Didn't one in the left ear indicate something, back in the day? That you were gay or something? Or has she just misunderstood that?

She knows a Danish man who wears one earring. The earring is made from his wedding ring. He got it made when he and his first wife divorced, because there is a proverbial expression where he comes from: 'May you wear that memory like a ring in your ear!' Now he has also become divorced from his second wife but he still wears the earring,

Mostly Linda loses one earring at a time. But sometimes – as now – a pair goes missing together, like a couple eloping or sneaking off on a clandestine weekend. Usually this happens when she's away somewhere herself, on a work trip, or on a holiday, in the days when she went on holidays. Before. She assumes she leaves them behind in the hotel, in the haste of packing. Or maybe they go astray in her luggage, although it's hard to figure out exactly how this might happen.

For the past while she has tried to be careful.

She established some earring rules.

1. Never take them off except when you are at home in your bedroom.
2. Don't put them in your handbag, in your make-up bag, or your pocket.

3. Don't go to bed in them and don't put them on the bedside locker.
4. Always put them in the box on the dressing table.

For about a year, everything seemed to go well. She has held on to four pairs – two pairs of dangly earrings that were good for special occasions or nights out, and two pairs of modest studs that she could wear for ordinary days. (Another thing about earrings. You have to wear them regularly. If you go without earrings for over a week, say, the holes in your ears start to close up and it hurts to stick earrings in them.)

A fortnight ago, the day she booked the flight to Lanzarote, she found she had no earrings at all, except for a pair of very long dangly ones, only suitable for dramatic occasions, and the precious amber earrings David had given her on their thirtieth wedding anniversary. They'd celebrated by going on a Baltic cruise. He bought the earrings in Tallinn, in Estonia, which was one of the cities the ship stopped at. In Tallinn there is a lovely little warren of streets full of craft shops of all kinds, glass makers and potters and weavers. Silversmiths. The amber was real. There was a small fly embalmed in one earring, and in the other, a scrap of leaf. Millions of years old. Both were set in thick twisted silver. 'You are a Viking princess!' David laughed, when he handed her the box. 'Or a Viking witch,' she responded. 'Only sometimes.' He kissed her and they walked hand in hand along the cobbled street – not a thing they did at home in Dublin, not any more.

The amber earrings were on the dressing table last night, in their black velvet box. She's sure of it. The box is still there, but the earrings aren't.

Although the taxi will call in half an hour, she starts searching.

High and low. (Mostly low.)

She looks under her big bed and pulls it out.

She empties the drawer under the bed, a dangerous spot, stuffed with tights, socks (many also odd, but she wears mismatched socks, at least in boots), underwear, and various stray items. She looks carefully at the places where she might have absentmindedly left earrings – the bookshelf beside the sofa, the mantelpiece, the television table, the little table in the bathroom. Also, under the sofa, under the bookshelves, under the rugs.

Although time is running out she goes out onto the street and checks the car, in the pocket in the door that's full of old bills, sweets, half-eaten bars of chocolate, coins for the supermarket trolley, old keys.

Three years ago, David was coming home from a conference in New York. As usual, after these trips, Linda was at the airport to pick him up. David would happily have taken the bus but she missed him when he was away, even for a few days or a week, and she loved the ritual of driving to the airport, standing in the arrivals hall, waiting for the glass doors to slide back. For her those sliding doors never lost their magic – she loved the way they opened like curtains on a stage, to reveal the travellers, pushing their trolleys, stepping out of that liminal zone between away and home. She loved the moment when David would emerge, smiling, looking all around. He never spotted her, or anyone; he was tall, and also very impractical, a typical absent-minded professor. His eyes scanned the whole hall, but he always looked at the air above her head, above everyone's head, the space between the scalps and the ceiling. She'd give him a few seconds, then go over and hug him as he came through the gap in the barrier that cordoned off the doors. Hey. Welcome back. How was it?

On this occasion – it was also springtime, it was the week before Easter – he didn't appear. She waited for half an hour. There can be delays, luggage missing. David was not good at answering his mobile; it was not switched on. As usual. Then a fuss, a shocked hush over the people waiting at the barrier. An ambulance crew, carrying a stretcher. She felt her heart tighten. Not that she knew, at the moment the doors slid open and the stretcher came out – although later, when she was telling the story, she revised, dramatised: she often said, 'At that moment, I knew.' In any case it wasn't long till she found out, from a woman in uniform – probably police uniform, she couldn't remember – who followed the stretcher. Followed the corpse: David was already dead. He had collapsed at the luggage belt, waiting for his bag to come around. (They delivered it to the house a week later. By then he was already buried.)

You never got to say goodbye was a thing several people said, sympathetically, over the next months. Did they really think that would have made much difference? The sympathisers had a tendency to focus on circumstances surrounding the death, rather than the death itself, and what it meant. As if they couldn't face up to the fact or the word 'death', and were batting it away with comments on related topics. The wolf death, the wolf widowhood, fended off with a flapping hand. 'At least it was quick.'

It's hard to talk about death. Nonexistence is not a thing you can imagine – the best you can do is dwell on the circumstances, or pretend death doesn't really happen. For a long time after David's death, Linda felt like a small animal, a small starved cat, or a mouse. A spider. Rattling around in the house is the phrase people use. Not lonely, at first. Loneliness is a state in which you crave human companionship. Linda didn't particularly want the companionship of other people, in that first year, or two. The only person she wanted was the one she could not get.

This longing was desperate, like the longing of a child for its mother; somehow she could remember the feeling, from long ago, about sixty years ago – the deep deep sadness, mixed with terror, if her mother was away for any length of time, if her mother was sick. Maybe that's why she felt small?

After about three years she thought about David less often. The feeling she got then could not be described as happiness. When people asked – the people who remembered, and who were not afraid to raise old ghosts – she would say 'Fine. Better. You get used to it.'

For that first year or two she was waiting for David to come back – this is what widows wait for even though they know it can't happen. Their bodies and hearts refuse to listen to their minds. But then she started waiting for other things, possible things. The next thing, whatever it happened to be. A film with a friend. A trip abroad. Mourning was replaced by restlessness: life became a series of stepping-stones, a frog-hop from one to the next, a journey to some mysterious unknown shore. Gradually it occurred to her that she might never get there, to that shore. It was possible that she might never feel happy again, in the old sense – content, comfortable in the moment, in the everyday. But still – not feeling actively unhappy was enough to be going on with.

*

Three years after David's death, Linda's restlessness took a new turn. She decided she would sell their house, and move. Make a new start. She rang an estate agent and in no time at all it was on the market. Twice a week Linda had to go for a walk or a drive, and leave her house under the control of the estate agent, who showed people around. The rule seemed to be that these people, who might buy her house, should never come face to face with her, the owner.

But one Sunday morning she met a couple at the gate of the house. They were hovering on the footpath, looking at the garden.

'I viewed the house last week,' the woman said, apologetically. 'Viewed' is the word for this activity, not 'looked at'. 'I just wanted to show it to my husband. We go for a walk along here, often.'

'Would you like to come in?' They didn't look like people who were going to tie her up and murder her once they got inside the door.

Diffidently, they followed her up the drive and into the hall. A couple, about the same age as she was.

'You have a beautiful house,' the woman said. She said it with conviction. Linda was surprised. 'Do you think so?'

'It's unusual. Most houses look the same. I've seen a lot. But this one ... the size of the rooms.'

'The garden of course,' said Linda.

'Even apart from that.' The woman looked around the hall, a square hall, with a golden floor and winding staircase. 'It's special.'

'Thank you,' said Linda.

The next day, she rang the estate agent and took the house off the market.

Instead of moving, she made renovations.

*

What Linda knew was that David would not have wanted her to move. But he would not have approved of the renovations either. What he would definitely have disliked was her disposing of his books.

They had been upstairs, downstairs, in the sitting room, and in the study. Six thousand of them. The house was more like a library than an ordinary home.

Now his books have been in boxes, in a steel container in a storage place in Tallaght, for a year and a half, waiting for a real library to come and take them. They need to be released. They need to breathe – literally. It's not good for volumes to be packed together, pressed on top of one another, in confined dark, cold spaces. Books need air.

Over the past few weeks, when all the earrings vanished, she began to wonder if David was taking her earrings to express his displeasure at the way she is treating his books. If she had left everything alone the books would be comfortably accommodated on the fine shelves he had built all over the house, or in the big study he had made in the converted garage – it was soon to be a new apartment, which Linda would let on Airbnb.

But the books have been in storage for ages. Wouldn't he have started protesting about them before now?

It can't be the books.

Could it be Lars?

She had met Lars at a book launch, which was lucky, because most people at book launches are women. He is the Dane, who wears the tiny earring in his left ear. She didn't fall in love with him but she could have a conversation with him. They had gone out several times, to dinner, to the occasional play or movie. He kissed her goodnight but it was in the manner of everyone, the modern way, the book launch way, not the dating way. He seemed to accept that there would be nothing more, that they were just good friends, which suited her fine. She was getting used to him. It went on for a few months.

Then a month ago he told her he was going back to Denmark to visit his children – he was divorced, he had two grown-up sons, and grandchildren.

'How nice!' Linda said. 'How long will you be away?'

Three months.

This announcement was made over dinner, in an old restaurant with plush red velvet banquettes, and nooks and crannies. Dripping candles on the tables, and chandeliers hanging low from the ceiling.

Lars looked her in the eye.

'It has been nice, getting to know you.'

Nothing about staying in touch. Nothing about see you when I get back. Not to mention, would you like to come to Denmark for a weekend?

Breaking it off?

That was when she changed her mind about her ability to fall in love. Or to have feelings of some kind, for a man who was not David.

Missing Lars was not like missing men she was in love with when she was young, nothing as overwhelming as that. And not like missing David. But there was something, all right … and she allowed herself to go with the feeling. She allowed herself to think about him.

That was in January.

There was no word from him in February or March. Then she sent a neutral email, to which he responded, 'All well here. Very cold.'

Then in the second week of April he emailed and

suggested a short holiday. 'I have had enough of the snow. Would you join me in the Canaries for a few days, or a week, after Easter?' Which was late that year. Easter.

Did David take the earrings because he doesn't want her to go to Lanzarote?

But she doesn't believe in any of this. And neither does David. Dead or alive he would not believe it. He was a folklorist. Some people think a folklorist is a person who tells fairytales, who wears a funny old cap, who believes in all kinds of superstitious rubbish. But a folklorist is someone who reads ten languages, who studies the traditions and cultures of people all over the world, who has a scientific and analytic mind. A folklorist understands why people believe in fairies and ghosts and other supernatural beings (gods, God) but a folklorist rarely believes in any of this stuff himself. He knows too much about variation, about illusion, about how belief interacts with fact to sustain illusion.

It works like this: if you 'believe' in ghosts, and you catch a glimpse of a sheet flapping in the wind, near a graveyard, or hear the clanking of something that sounds like chains, you will fill in the fact (a shadowy white cloth, a sound) with the belief. A sheet becomes a fairy. A rattling gate becomes a dead man walking.

The human imagination transforms a missing earring to a sign. It interprets it whatever way it likes. But a missing earring is just a missing earring. Always.

In bed, in the middle of the night, she wakes up, remembering something.

'I found the earrings.'

'Yes, my darling. I knew you would find them.'

His voice is round, rich, good-humoured. Not sleepy.

'Look!'

She shows the earrings to him, in the dark – four pairs of earrings, a handful.

'That's wonderful, darling.'

Is he really there? She turns. Yes, the long hill of a body under the duvet, beside her. His head is on the pillow. His face is a little paler than usual, a little more defined and bony, and his hands, when she takes them, a little cold. She kisses him and kisses him. First with a bit of trepidation, a bit of resistance, as if he might have bad breath. But soon she falls into the kiss, and they kiss and kiss and hold one another tight.

So the stories are true. He has come back.

She sees him, she feels him, she hears him, their lips are touching.

Something rings inside her own body. A siren whispers.

And she shakes herself, deliberately. She thought she was awake. But she wasn't; now she is awake. And when she looks David is not there. She's alone in their big bed, on her side of it. The duvet on the other side is flat, his side of the bed is empty, just as it has been for the past four years. Of course it is. David is dead.

The stories are stories.

She falls asleep again, and dreams of him again, but this time in a real dream place, a kitchen rather like their kitchen and rather different from it, one of those familiar unfamiliar dream rooms. Now she's mopping the floor, and he comes in wearing his dressing gown and hugs and kisses her again. The kiss is even deeper and longer and better. But she knows where she stands, lying asleep, washing the floor of a room not quite like any she has ever been in, one of those familiar dream places.

She buys new earrings at the airport. Small, discreet, silver with mother-of-pearl, fake, insets – they will do, for the holiday in Lanzarote. (She's never been there. She likes sunshine holidays, but David drew the line at the Canaries. They had only gone to places of real historical interest, to him – places where the Greeks and the Romans had been, or the Vikings. There is always plenty to do in such countries, things to see. Temples and towers and museums. Like many people Linda believes (wrongly) that the Canaries have no real history, half imagines that they sprang out of the sea in the recent past as a fully-fledged holiday resort. She wonders how she and Lars will spend the days, in this museum-less place. Four days. There'll be lots of time for lounging about. Yes.)

At the gate, waiting for the boarding announcement, she takes out a silk pouch in which she keeps her passport and credit cards when she's on the plane, to make sure she doesn't leave them behind – she can wear it around her neck, on a string, the way keyhole children used to carry the key of the door.

The amber earrings fall out, into her lap.

Now why would she have put them there, of all places?

She can think of reasons.

More than one.

Berlin

One Thursday the Wall comes down. Not literally. But the gates open, the guards leave their posts, anyone who feels like it can walk from one side of Berlin to the other. Lolly and Bill and Ryan and Gisela, their little German daughter, watch the event on the RTÉ news in their cottage in Stoneybatter. On the screen are crowds dancing and laughing and singing. Violins. She hums along. *Freude Freude*. She has an impression of candlelight, lanterns, soft festive flickerings, as at a summer garden party. It is November.

Can it have been such a surprise? Some dramatic things happen out of the blue – plane crashes, lightning strikes, mass shootings in America. But not big political events. The process of liberation has been going on for years. Glasnost and perestroika have entered the English language, words as familiar as vodka or caviar. The kind-looking soft face of the Russian president was on TV every turn about. But Lolly has been so preoccupied – work, the children, the curtains in the bathroom – that she hasn't paid much attention to what was going behind the Iron Curtain, even though it has important implications for her, and even more for Gisela. The last thing you can imagine is a big public answer to a personal question, because, no matter how well you know the truth of it, it's hard to believe in your bones that the personal is political, and vice versa.

Exactly ten years earlier Lolly had been in Berlin. Nobody had had the slightest expectation then that the Wall was entering its last decade. Lolly thought it had been there for ages, since the end of the War, although in fact it had been erected in 1961. Already by 1979 it felt old and permanent. She was spending that year, the year between August '78 and '79, on a research scholarship in Copenhagen: the research was a history of a story that had first been documented by a German poet in the twelfth century and had since then been written and told by various writers and storytellers over most of Europe. The story was a fairy tale about an abandoned child; a bit like Hansel and Gretel, a scary story that ended well, being a fairy tale, but that contained metaphorical references to infanticide, child exposure and such unspeakable customs, widely practised in the days when people had no birth control. She had acquired versions of the story from archives all over Europe – thick shiny photocopies with the pungent chemical smell photocopies had in the 1970s. But there was a version she hadn't managed to get, in the Humboldt Library in East Berlin. Her letters had not been answered. Since she knew a girl who was studying in West Berlin, she decided to visit her and the divided city, and check the reference in person.

At Friedrichstrasse railway station she went through the Wall, which wasn't actually a wall at that point, just several little grey booths, like ticket offices, where they scrutinised your passport and quizzed you about the purpose of your visit, before finally deciding whether or not to let you through. Half an hour later she was in the library.

The Humboldt Library had high ceilings, sculpted friezes and a general air of untidiness. It was very unlike the big new library in West Berlin, but quite similar to the National Library in Dublin. As in Dublin, there were reference books around the walls but you had to order most books at the librarian's desk, and wait for them to be delivered by an attendant. Lots of staff then, checking tickets and dockets, fetching and carrying. A certain amount of hanging about, waiting. At the long table the readers were bent over their books, engrossed. As in every library of this kind there was a harmonious hum of activity – the music of reading, of writing notes. You could almost hear the minds in conversation with the texts.

She found her reference and handed in her docket at the big oak desk. The volume came soon enough, within ten minutes, and yes, there was the story, on page 151. Wouldn't it have been easy for them to get it and send a copy? But she was glad they hadn't, because it was nice to have a reason for coming here, to East Berlin. For her, as for most people, it felt better to be a tourist with a purpose than an idle *flâneur*.

She read the story. Easy now in any of the several languages it occurs in – stories need no passports, they pass linguistic and political borders as easily as a shower of rain. A virus. The plot she knew like the back of her hand. A hungry father decides he has to get rid of his youngest child. He gives her to a woodcutter, who is to kill her and hide the body. But the woodcutter just dumps the child in the forest to be eaten by wild animals. A prince happens to ride by and he rescues the babe, who grows up to be a beauty, and so on and so forth. The details could vary – oral storytellers tended to stick to the point, whereas the writers padded out the story with descriptions of weather, landscape, costume. Even in these superfluous details there was a surprising amount of uniformity: the writers were shameless copycats.

She asked about photocopying at the counter. The librarian directed her to another room, pointing to a grey door. She went through the door. A dark corridor stretched in front of her. Empty. Along she went and turned a corner. Now she was in a dim room with no windows, where newspapers were piled high in untidy stacks, from floor to ceiling. Ancient iron shelves were weighted with hundreds of books, bound in old worn brown leather and green leather. There was a strong smell of musty paper, and of something else. Old wood. Or little animals. Mice?

She was sure she shouldn't be in this place.

The room had two doors. They both looked exactly the same: they had been painted green, aeons ago, and looked as if they were covered in lichen. She opened one of the doors and found herself in a corridor. It was lined with stacks – mountains – of old books, pamphlets, newspapers. They looked as if they'd been there since the Middle Ages. But towards the end of this passage was a huge modern thing, a monstrous machine. So maybe, miraculously, she had followed the librarian's directions properly? Maybe this was the photocopier?

She opened the lid and placed her book upside down on the glass plate.

She pushed a button.

Nothing happened.

Pushed another button.

Nothing happened.

Pushed it again, harder.

The machine emitted a loud roar, like a lawnmower starting up. The roar got louder and louder. She smelled something burning. No smoke but the machine sounded as if it were about to explode. She grabbed the book – possibly the only copy of this work in the world – and backed away.

A young man came running down the corridor, waving his arms and shouting.

Was machen Sie?

Ein fotokopie.

Warum?

He snatched the book from her hand. He examined it swiftly and then pulled a plug out of a socket in the wall. The machine gradually stopped roaring, and, after a few whimpers, lapsed into silence.

The man glared.

Das ist kaput. Und lebensgefährlich.

To her surprise, without any warning, tears started running down her cheeks.

He was also surprised. And dismayed.

What do you want? In English. More sympathetically.

I just want a photocopy. Of this fairy tale.

He was tall and fair-haired, but his eyes were dark, and – now – soft. What was he wearing? A green shirt, a tie, some sort of grey trousers.

He led her to an office where a woman with a big bun of bright red hair and thick glasses, wearing a pink cardigan, guarded a more modern-looking photocopier.

Teresa!

Lolly filled in a form. Teresa checked her passport and her day visitor's visa and her ticket for the library. All this before she was allowed to get a copy of a fairy tale written down in 1812. Plus fifteen marks, five for the copy and ten for the postage.

Teresa would send it on, in three weeks, or four weeks. No guarantees.

Danke, Teresa.

Then, she didn't know how to get back to the Reading Room, how to escape from the library into the streets of East Berlin.

'I will show you,' said the librarian. His name, she had heard from Teresa, was Gerhardt.

They sat in a cafe on Unter den Linden. He told her a great deal about himself. He had an MA in Slavonic languages. Russian and Bulgarian. He translated novels from Bulgarian and went to Bulgaria on holiday. Another surprise. Communist holidays.

'I've never heard of a Bulgarian writer.'

'The most famous one is Ivan Vasov.'

'Have you translated him?'

He didn't laugh when he explained that Vasov was a nineteenth-century author whose work had been translated many times already. Gerhardt did contemporary writers, for the money.

'Do they pay well?' The question was out before she could stop it. Obviously not. This was a communist state.

'It's adequate. It's extra. And I could work at it full time.'

So there were actual jobs, in publishing companies, for translators? Full-time jobs.

'I would like to translate from English. An Irish writer perhaps. Who would you recommend?'

Lolly could never think of anything when asked questions like that. Can you recommend a good restaurant in Dublin? Which Irish writer should I read? She read novels all the time, and was familiar with many Irish writers. But who was best? Who could you recommend, safely, to a foreigner?

'Aidan Higgins?' she just about remembered the name of one of his books. But once she started thinking several names came to mind. The new writers she knew of were mostly women. She took it for granted that he would want to translate male writers.

'John McGahern, some people like him. John Banville.' She thought. 'William Trevor.'

He got her to write the names in his notebook.

The sun began to sink and the air to grow cold and they were still talking. The lights came on, the quiet lights of the East and the glaring lights of the West. When it was time to go, before the gate closed, he asked if she had a boyfriend.

The question made her stomach somersault.

'Sort of.'

He pulled her close to him. They were walking back to the Wall, hand in hand.

She decided not to ask him the same question but he answered it anyway.

'I have a girlfriend. And a baby. On the way. '

'Well.'

He gave her a quick kiss on the mouth, and she went back to the West, through the Wall.

The year abroad that had seemed eternal was dashing to its end. In September she'd have to go back to Ireland. It had to happen. She had a boyfriend, she had a family, she had friends. But she didn't want to go back. She avoided the word 'home'. Although it wasn't a word she could apply to Denmark either, obviously; what she loved about

Denmark was mainly that it was not home, but 'away': she loved the unfamiliarity of it, as well as the taste of its Viennese pastries and potted herrings and rye bread, the curl of its language in her ears, the pragmatism of the people. The snow and frozen sea in winter and now the hot summer. When she thought of Ireland her stomach sank – the old sow who eats her farrow. It was reaching out for her with big fat crubeens, it would drag her in to its drab ordinariness, its dull jobs, its army of priests and nuns, its relentless mediocrity. So it seemed. (She was twenty-two. She took Joyce too seriously.)

The day after she came back to Dublin the Pope arrived. All her old college friends went to the Phoenix Park, with bottles of champagne, to celebrate the visit of the great man. They clapped and cheered as he encouraged them to maintain the faith. Oh yes! 'Faith of Our Fathers, Holy Faith,' they sang, lustily. Girls who had been on the pill for years, girls who had gone to England for abortions, sang at the tops of their voices in the golden September sunshine. 'Young people of Ireland, I love you.'

If only he knew what they were really like.

How she longed to be back in Copenhagen, where people could think straight.

Gerhardt sent the first letter when she had been back in Dublin a few weeks. She responded and posted some novels by newish Irish writers to him.

Months passed, before the next letter. And then, some years.

Lolly and Bill – the boyfriend – moved in together. They bought a house, they married. They had a baby, Ryan.

He was one and a half when Gerhardt wrote to say he

would come on a visit.

Lolly had to explain who he was, and why they should welcome him to their home.

'He rescued me once,' she said. 'From a monster, in a library.'

'They're everywhere. Even in libraries.'

'It was a machine, not a human.'

Bill raised an eyebrow.

'A photocopying machine.'

'They have minds of their own, photocopiers. Mean minds.'

'So I owe him,' she spoke firmly.

But as well as believing she owed him one, she was worried. What if he was trying to escape, to the West? She had always suspected his motives in keeping in touch.

'If he was defecting he'd pick somewhere better than here.'

The attraction might be freedom?

'Freedom from what? He's probably doing just what he says. Getting a sense of place, or context, or whatever. For the book. Who wrote it anyway?'

'James Joyce.'

So much for contemporary.

'He'll have to sleep on the sofa,' Lolly said.

That's where guests slept – her mother, usually. It wasn't very comfortable, in the small, dark sitting room.

'But he'd be used to that sort of thing, I suppose, in the GDR.'

'Won't the publisher give him some money for a hotel? Or a hostel? They must have some money, even there. How long does he say he's staying for?'

'Four weeks.'

'Jesus, Mary and Joseph!'

*

In front of the gate in arrivals she waited. Ryan was with her, on a rein, since he could move fast when he wanted to.

'Plane', he said. 'Plane.' He sounded cross, as he scanned the boring arrivals lounge, looking for a plane.

'Yes, it's coming, soon.'

'Plane.'

He repeated his new words ad nauseam, apparently making sure he locked each in his mind before moving on to the next one. For the first weeks after he had started saying words, she had kept notes in a special notebook with a bright blue cover. Baba. Bottle. Bow wow. But as his vocabulary increased she lost track. She also lost the notebook.

Actually the plane had already landed. Passengers were coming through the grey door that opened dramatically, like a curtain on a stage, the gateway through which you passed from the no-man's-land of the airport into the land of Ireland. In those days you could try to guess where travellers were coming from by their appearance, their clothes. The first lot through included several people in summer outfits, beach clothes ... shorts, flip-flops. (It was raining outside and about fourteen degrees.) Then men in suits with briefcases. From Heathrow, clearly. Then two young women wearing close-fitting tweed jackets, beige trousers that looked like jodhpurs, and gleaming brown boots.

They must be the passengers from the Düsseldorf plane.

She had forgotten what Gerhardt looked like. She'd been in love with him for an afternoon, in a cafe on Unter den Linden, and she had cherished the memory of those hours for years, but not seriously, more like a postcard of some pleasant place she visited than as a precious gift she could not be parted from. The details were blurred, to put it mildly. Blonde hair, curly, a sweet smile. He was taller than she was, she remembered that from their walk to the Wall, but so were most German men. What colour were his eyes? (Well, there were only a few possibilities.) She couldn't have identified him in a police line-up.

She was pretty sure he wouldn't recognise her either, so she had prepared a little sign. Her name, Lolly, written in red marker on a piece of A3 paper, with 'Welcome Gerhardt!' underneath.

'Gimme ice cream.'

Sometimes she was thrilled when Ryan managed to put a few words together, to form a sentence, even if it was always in the imperative mood.

'Shut up.'

He was startled by the tone, even though he didn't know what the words meant.

'Excuse me!'

The bright high voice of an air hostess. Had she overheard? The Aer Lingus hostess, in her green suit, tight skirt, perky pillbox hat. With the smooth beige face and an accusing smile.

'Sorry?'

'Are you Mrs Lolly Moore?'

She nodded at the bit of paper with the names. Lolly and Gerhardt.

She was holding a little girl by the hand. Blond curly hair, brown eyes.

That was Gisela, Gerhardt's daughter.

'We can't just keep her.'

'Why not?'

Gisela had, in her pathetic plastic communist suitcase, a West German passport, and a birth certificate. The EU rules had changed. You didn't need a visa or a permit to live in Ireland if you were an EU citizen.

'She's not an EU citizen.'

'Her passport says she is.'

'*Jawohl.*'

She also had a letter, from someone called Dieter Hartmann: 'Gerhardt could not get out. He wants you to look after Gisela until he can join her in a week or two.'

There was a telephone number and an address in West Berlin.

So of course they kept her. Gisela.

Just a few weeks, it was at the beginning.

Gerhardt could not get out for some complicated reason – someone in his family, someone who was not Gisela, had done something wrong, so his travel permit was cancelled. They didn't care about his translation of James Joyce. He'd just have to do it without visiting Dublin and getting a sense of the story settings.

So Gisela stayed. A month. Two months. Nobody who mattered asked serious questions. Lolly had lived abroad for over a year, Bill was a writer. In Stoneybatter, which had not yet been yuppified, they were regarded as slightly eccentric. They didn't clean their windows. Obviously they were the sort of people who could have friends in Germany – or anywhere – who would die or be shot or something and ask them to look after their child.

It was easier than you'd think. Easier than it should be.

And now the Wall is down. Gerhardt can go wherever he likes. The world is his oyster.

Free travel all over the globe, or at least all over the EU (if you have the money).

Gisela has not forgotten her father, or presumably her mother. She is ten now. She cannot have forgotten anything significant, especially any journey or change of location that she has experienced since she was two or three. Of her parents, their home, East Berlin and how they got her out of it, she must have distinct and clear memories.

But she never talks about any of that. She talks, in English, which she learnt fast, about school, her pals in Dublin, the TV shows she likes.

She's a bright and charming child. Everyone loves her.

Especially Lolly.

Gerhardt will obviously contact them. He will probably show up unannounced, on the doorstep, and claim his daughter, citizen of the free world. Any day now.

'Maybe Gisela isn't Gerhardt's child at all?' Bill comes up with this. 'She had a false passport.'

But if she is not Gerhardt's, then who is she?

You mean, whose is she?

There is a nursery rhyme that Lolly learnt when she was over there, in Denmark, the year she went down to Berlin on the train. 1979.

> Lille kat
> Lille kat
> Lille kat på vejen
> Hvis er du?
> Hvis er du?
> Jeg er sku min ejen.

Lolly recites it to Gisela sometimes, in a loose translation.

Little cat
Little cat
Little cat in the tree.
Whose are you?
Whose are you?
I belong to me.

Bill does not know this rhyme, of course.

'She's ours, I suppose. Until further notice' is what he says. And Lolly is happy with that, for now.

The Kingfisher Faith

The plane landed in Dublin at 8 a.m. The grey morning air touched Ciara's skin like cold water. Queensland had been too hot. But there was a joyousness in the burning sun and the clear skies, the children swimming on riverside beaches in the middle of the city. It lightened the heart. Ciara had felt deliciously weightless in the warm, bright air – she had imagined herself a bird, a migratory bird, a swallow, sailing swiftly above her own life. Back to earth now. When all is said and done, Ireland is a melancholy land. It's not surprising that so many people emigrate. They cite economic reasons but that's not the whole story. The young Irish in Australia say they miss home but add that they like the weather in Queensland, or Victoria, or wherever they happen to find themselves on that distant continent. If they like the weather, chances are they're never coming back.

When she gave her address to the taxi man, he asked her an unusual question: 'Have you lived there long?'

'I've lived there for twenty-five years.'

He was surprised. It turned out he lived there too, when he was twenty. Since then he's moved five times. 'Chock-a-block with bedsits in those days,' he said. 'That's all changed, of course.'

He complained at some length about planners and the housing policy of the government, and homelessness. 'I'm not against immigrants,' he went on. 'We were immigrants ourselves for long enough, weren't we? But they're getting flats and houses when young Irish people are left on the street ... or on the sofa of their mother's gaffe. I was giving a lift to a family from Nigeria the other day. From the airport. They'd been to the Canaries on a holiday.' He pauses, to let her consider the significance of this fact. 'And where did they live? A semi-detached, four-bedroom house in Blanchardstown.' Pause. Sigh. 'My son has a wife and two children and he's in a flat outside Ballymun paying fifteen hundred euro a month ... before ESB or anything. There's something wrong. I've nothing against them but there's something wrong.'

Ciara didn't bother trying to change the subject. She stopped listening.

Her cat, Percy, was in the garden, waiting.

Usually reserved and aloof, Percy was delighted to see Ciara, and rubbed his smooth, silky fur against her leg until food was offered. He looked fine – Mary next door had obviously looked after him well. Ciara made the cup of coffee for which she had been longing for hours, and began to open her letters. Bills. Good news comes by email, bills in the post. There were two marked 'Confidential. Only to be opened by the addressee.' When she opened the envelope she saw the BREAST CHECK logo on the letterhead. She had completely forgotten that she had had the routine mammogram just before she left for Brisbane, a month ago. They always wrote a week or two later to say everything was all right.

But not this time.

There was a recall for a second investigation. There were three envelopes and three letters, in fact. They'd written three times.

So.

A leaflet accompanied the letter, including information. A call-back does not mean anything is wrong, it murmured reassuringly. Then it described what would happen on the second visit. Another mammogram, an ultrasound scan, and possibly a biopsy using a needle. (There were a few different kinds of needle, some more unpleasant than others, Ciara guessed.) You may be more comfortable in a skirt and blouse or trousers and blouse, it said, and asked people who used perfume or deodorant (deodorant? Are there women who don't use deodorant?) not to put on too much of either. Prepare to stay in the clinic for three hours. You may bring someone with you.

You are supposed to arrive at the clinic at 8.15 a.m. Another early start. The Dublin Horse Show is on. It is Ladies' Day, the day when women in remarkable hats compete to win the 'Best Dressed Lady' competition, so there is plenty of traffic on the M50. But Ciara manages to arrive at 8.30.

The Breast Check Clinic is familiar – she's been here, over the years, at least half a dozen times. It's a nice place, considering it is part of a hospital, a hospital where you don't have to pay a few hundred euro for a five-minute chat with a doctor. The colour scheme is white with touches of sky blue, always guaranteed to produce a sense of freshness. The magazines on the tables – *Country Life, Image, Vogue* – are up to date, unlike the magazines in any other waiting room Ciara has ever been in. The staff are well mannered, kind and thoughtful. Today, however, this kindness is a mixed blessing. The receptionist greets her with a gentle smile, doesn't ask her to produce any documents.

Doesn't even ask her to spell her name.

Nobody can spell Ciara's surname, because it's in Irish, something which most Irish officials find baffling, as if Ciara has chosen it for the express purpose of annoying them.

This person obviously knows something.

Whenever Ciara has been here before there have been only a few other women waiting. But today the front foyer is full – full of women, and not a few men. The husbands, the boyfriends. No doubt sisters and daughters and mothers and female friends too, but you can't distinguish them from the patients at this point in the proceedings. Everybody looks solemn, but nobody is freaking out. In fact nobody is even talking. The place is as silent as the tomb. Are all the silent women people who have got the second letter, calling them back? Or are there women on their third or fourth test, women who actually have got cancer? Probably not, she thinks. Probably they are all in the same boat. The second-letter folk.

One in twenty gets called back, according to the leaflet.

That's not a comforting statistic. Nineteen times out of twenty – nine and a half times out of ten – everything looks fine, on the mammograms. In this room are the 5 per cent who failed the test.

Still. The statistic for survival is pretty good. Even of women who are diagnosed with breast cancer, 85 per cent survive (for five years). Five years, which would include a lot of hassle in the form of chemotherapy, radiotherapy, hair loss. And so on.

And what if it has already jumped around to other places in your body? Then you could have a month.

Her left breast certainly feels a bit peculiar. There's an itchy spot underneath, and the nipple feels rather stiff. (These symptoms occurred for the first time this morning, on the M50, when she was driving to the hospital.)

She would have to get a wig. Well, okay. Friends who had gone through the treatment looked good in their wigs, frequently better than they'd looked with their real hair. Wigs were thick and shiny, like the hair of teenagers. Hot, but that wouldn't be much of a problem in Ireland, and she wouldn't be going back to Australia, or anywhere else, if she were having chemo. And as for going to bed … nobody ever sees her in bed any more.

Actually, the more she thinks about it, the less she cares about the treatment, or even about dying. Her life is fine. It's often enjoyable. But she doesn't really mind all that much if it ends.

The separation from Bobby had to happen. They had been quarrelling for years, they'd stopped having sex ages ago. The parting had been by mutual agreement, and amicable enough. When they finally split up, when he moved out, Ciara's main feeling had been of relief. It's over, I can move on.

He moved in with someone else very quickly. The someone was a man. This is the sort of thing that happens in soap operas, Ciara thought. It's ridiculous, it's unbelievable, it's crazy. Bobby is not gay. But maybe he's what they used to call AC/DC? They were an item, Bobby and his man. Not just housemates.

Ciara didn't want him back. Not at all. But she did

want something: the past. What she wanted was history. The life she – and he – had had when they were starting off, when he was in love with her and she with him. If she longed for anything, it was that time of being in love. When she had felt like a sparkling river running over rocks in the sun, or like white clouds in the blue sky. When all her heavy human body of blood and flesh and bone had been transformed to something light, like a sonata or a song. To the south wind blowing. That's what being in love was like. Something that surpassed all understanding, that subsumed you, but that you could not find words to describe. It was the best life had to offer. All, she was pretty sure, it had to offer. All that matters.

Fleeting, the time of love. It is fleeting no matter what. Even if your partner stays with you forever, those times of glad grace, transcendence, don't come again.

Otherwise, what is there?

Sex. The sea and the garden and what's for dinner. My books. My music. My friends.

Soon I may no longer exist. But how can anyone get their head around that huge but evanescent idea, the idea of their own non-being? That's a thought that is as hard to catch as love. A thought that is also as elusive as a cloud, water in a sieve. It's the very essence of the unthinkable.

People are always saying – people in newspapers, people on radio shows, people of that sort – that we should spend more time thinking about death. But as far as Ciara can figure out, it's impossible to think about it at all. You can think around it, but you can't imagine death itself. Much easier to imagine what it will be like to live on Mars, or what it might have been like to be a Stone Age man, woman or child. Or animal. But your own non-being? Your own 'not I'? You could as easily imagine what a stone feels, or a bone, or a pound of butter. She has concluded that the only sensible way to deal with death is the one most people employ. Namely, ignore the damn thing.

Maybe the prospect of death feels different if your partner is still with you. Yes. It must do. Having a partner still with you would be both a blessing and a curse. A, you don't want to leave them, and B, you have to worry about how they'll feel when you do.

He has found someone else, but she hasn't. And just as well. Now, when she's dying of cancer, she won't have to say goodbye to someone who shares her life and they won't have to say goodbye to her. These partings, of the living and the dead, are not sweet sorrow. They are deep and searing sorrow, ghastly sorrow, which you would only wish upon your very worst enemy. But hey. Nobody will be devastated when Ciara sheds off the mortal coil. Good! A few people will be sad for a while, probably – well, she hopes so. Her children, her grandchildren. Her sister and brother? Maybe a friend or two. Nobody will be sorry overmuch. So she has one less thing to worry about. In fact, when you think about it, just as she's free to come and go on holidays, or to do up the house, or hop on a plane to Brisbane, she's free to die. Free as a bird. Freer, because dying is free – it's the one big trip everyone can afford, although some go economy and some business class.

The women are called in batches of three or four for the first examination. Everyone looks up expectantly when the nurse comes in with the names and everyone looks at the women who turn the corner and disappear. What awaits them, around that corner?

Another waiting room. That's what.

146

First you go to a little cubicle, take off your blouse and bra, and replace them with an enormous blue smock. You put your clothes and bag into a basket, and, clutching this and the flap of the smock, go to the second waiting room. This is also quite crowded. Ciara gets one of the last seats, facing the other women. So she can have a good look at them. Most are between fifty and sixty. Well, they'd have to be, since they don't start doing the breast check until you're fifty. Their shoes or sandals, sticking out from under the gowns: tasteful sandals, flat or almost flat, leather, the two band sandals that have been fashionable for the past two years and – in Ciara's opinion – suit most women very well. She has a pair herself although she's wearing shoes at the moment. The women have neat, casual hairstyles, lightly made-up faces. A few are reading actual books, while others look at the magazines – again – or at the TV in the corner. Nobody talks. Twenty-odd women, wearing identical sky-blue gowns, waiting for the second breast check, and not a word from any of them. It would not be so silent in the Mater, on the other side of the city, Ciara guesses.

She passes the time by learning a poem off by heart. Swallow, swallow, swallow, the poem starts. Teach me how to fly high in the sky so that summer will begin. Teach me your songs so that I can spend my days in the meadows and the hills, so that I can fly up to the stars. The poem is for children, by a Spanish poet, and it is in Spanish. It's a very simple poem but it's challenging to memorise it. She has to repeat the lines dozens and dozens of times, and still she tends to stumble on one of them. That I may spend my days like you is the line that trips her up, again and again. It's expressed rather awkwardly, to force a rhyme.

'Girls!' This nurse addresses them as 'Girls!' And it has

begun to feel like school here. Uniformed, single sex, waiting for a test — a viva.

Ciara is concentrating so hard on the poem that she almost forgets why she is here. Which is the point, which is why she decided to do this. Partly because she's concentrating and partly because she's tired, she doesn't seem to be especially worried, as far as she can tell.

The fact is, she doesn't believe there is anything wrong with her. But she barely expresses that thought even in the privacy of her mind. Tempting fate. And then … maybe she is just doing what people do. Denying. The first stage for patients with a fatal illness, according to Elizabeth Kubler Ross, is denial. The next is bargaining. She forgets what the others are … except for the final one. Acceptance.

Take it on the chin, shut up, kick the bucket.

But here comes stage two, or is it stage one — denial. I don't have it, I feel perfectly fine. Every single woman in this room is probably indulging in stage one denial, while doing a bit of stage two bargaining. You can very easily do both simultaneously. There is nothing wrong with me, and if there isn't something wrong I'll declutter the house from top to bottom and travel the world.

But for one in twenty there will be something wrong. That does not mean that nineteen of these women — there are about twenty — are going to escape. There could be something wrong with every single woman in this room, in their sky-blue smocks, with their silent, nicely made-up south County Dublin faces. These could be the unlucky percentile. While various other waiting rooms, scattered around the world, could be full to the brim of women whose tests will be clear. Statistics are tricky, and they only comfort the ones who are lucky.

A dark-haired woman, attractive — they are all fairly

attractive, considering the circumstances, but this one has that extra sparkle – comes in, carrying her basket. She giggles and says, 'Gosh, it's scary!' And there is a response. Of course. Everyone laughs and nods in agreement. The woman she sits beside exchanges a few words with her. Then all the women in the waiting room start chatting to one another. The garden of sky blue erupts into a symphony of gossip.

Monica Ryan.

Sibyl Freeman.

Geraldine Murphy.

Ciara is listening to the story of how Maura McGovern had got The Letter the day before she was going on holiday to Tuscany and agonised over whether or not to tell her husband when they call out her name.

'My name is Meg,' says the woman. 'I'm the radiographer.'

There's another mammogram.

'Just the right breast,' Meg says. She's rather bossy.

The itch in the left breast disappears, while its companion, the good right, is squashed like a pancake between the glass plates of the mammogram machine.

Then another wait in the same waiting room. Maura has vanished so Ciara goes over the poem again and manages to remember it in full. But her concentration is slipping. Why is she doing this?

An ultrasound scan.

'This will feel a bit cold,' the doctor says, 'but it won't hurt like the mammogram.'

'The mammogram didn't hurt either,' Ciara says. Then bites her tongue. She shouldn't have said that. The doctor looks offended. It used to hurt, Ciara hurries on apologetically, when I first came, it hurt, but not any more.

'I suppose you get used to it,' the doctor says. 'You're no longer afraid.'

And your breasts get flabbier. They don't try to fight back when squashed between two glass plates.

The ultrasound doesn't even feel very cold.

The doctor looks at the image on the screen.

Ciara looks too. A tangle of criss-crossed lines. She searches for a shadow, a disruption to the pattern. But it's double Dutch, this picture of the interior of her breast.

'Well ...'

'Oh!'

'There's something not quite clear.'

'Oh.'

'We'll do the biopsy, just to be on the safe side.'

'Okay.'

'There's probably nothing to worry about but something is not clear.'

'Right.'

'Emma will show you the way.'

And so, clutching the flap of her sky-blue smock and her plastic basket, she follows Emma to the next room, which is another waiting room.

After she had fed the cat and read the letters and drunk her coffee, she went for a short walk to get bread and milk at Bobby's Convenience Store. The shop is new – Bobby, from Pakistan, set it up a few years ago, providing a service that is very handy for everyone around here. It's located just beside a bridge that is centuries old, spanning the Tula river – more of a stream than a river, and not very well looked after. After its descent from the Dublin mountains it flows past blocks of apartments, housing estates; its banks are unkempt and littered. But in some places – Bobby's bridge is one – it is thickly overhung with shrubs and trees, and the water races along merrily through a lovely green tunnel of dappled leaves.

Just as Ciara crossed the bridge the sun came out. That's probably why she stopped and looked for a while down at the river, as it danced along in the bright light. Or maybe she stopped because she was remembering the Brisbane river, broad as a lake, festive with water buses and white yachts. Maybe that's why she looked into the little stream.

Then, the flash of blue.

Down the river, under the overhanging foliage, dashed the bird, quick as a swift, faster than a plane.

Kingfisher.

She had never seen one before. Never before in her life, and she is sixty-three years of age.

For five decades she had wanted to see one, but never has until this moment, on the bridge over the River Tula.

Douglas Hyde, first president of Ireland, adduced the kingfisher as a reason for believing in the fairies. How many people have seen a kingfisher? he asks, in an introduction to a book of fairy legends. And yet we believe they exist. So why not believe in the fairies?

It's logical. Up to a point.

Ciara has not believed in the fairies since she was ten years old, but she has always believed in the kingfisher. A kingfisher is not a fairy. But it is a rare wild bird, and to see one, even for the smallest particle of a second, is a great treat. And a particle of a second is all you'll get –the merest glimpse, a hint of a blue bird as lovely as a drop.

*

That's how it is, with wild things. You see them by chance. Whale-watching tours, dolphin tours mainly don't work. You see the whale when you're not looking for it, and the dolphin. That's what wild means. Wild cards, out of your control. They find you, generally when you least expect it.

Her heart rose, when she saw the kingfisher, the flash of blue in the golden green tunnel over the water.

She could still be surprised by joy.

It was, she thought, a good omen.

New Zealand Flax

The early purple orchids are plentiful this year. So plentiful that that Frida wonders if they really are as special and rare as she has always believed. In her field they're as common as the other flowers of June, the clover, the buttercups. The yellow one. Bird's-foot trefoil, sometimes called scrambled egg. Or, less meaningfully, bacon and eggs. Still, she swerves around any patch of grass graced by the chubby little orchids – turgid, phallic, episcopally purple – but mercilessly slices through buttercups and clover (which latter is the bees' favourite thing, and which smells nicer than the orchids, when the sun shines.) Little islands of long grass with an orchid or two or six dot the 'lawn' – that's not the right name for it. The patch of field that she cuts, so it's like a pond of short grass in a forest of long rough stuff.

'Why don't you get someone to do it?' Her son is exasperated on the phone. Perhaps a tad guilty? He hasn't been down here in over a year, to cut grass or do anything else. It's time to paint the walls, and the windows, and he likes doing that. He says. 'You shouldn't be going all the way down there just to *cut the grass*.'

'I'll get somebody,' she says. 'Before I leave.'

She has figured out, recently, that the best way of dealing with advice from him, or anyone, is to pretend to take it. Some people realise this when they're four years old, but better late than never.

The thing is. Having to cut the grass provides her with a reason for coming down. That's why she doesn't get a boy or a man to do it. That, and the cost, although it would most likely cost less than the price of the petrol for the drive down and back. And then, a man or a boy on one of the lawnmowers that look like toy tractors would not avoid the early purple orchids, or the two little hydrangea bushes, or the clumps of New Zealand flax that she planted last year and that have survived the winter storms, the spring storms, and the early summer storms. *Barely* survived. The spikes of flax look like the soldiers who came home from the trenches, battered, their skin burnt, and minus a couple of limbs. A man or a boy speeding around the field on a big lawnmower would certainly cut them down. A man or a boy wouldn't even see them.

Well. There is only one other person on earth who would see those clumps of pathetic flax.

Did she think, *on earth*?

She wipes the wheels and puts the lawnmower back in the garage. Just come and take a look, would you. When the sun goes down.

The lawnmower feels wounded. It has been rattled – the grass was more than a foot high; no ordinary lawnmower should have to deal with such stuff; it was a job for a big lump of farm machinery, a combine harvester maybe.

The blade may have loosened. After two hours pushing

against the gradient, the last thing Frida wants to do is examine the insides of the lawnmower. But she forces herself to take a look.

Yes. There is a screw loose on one of the wheels. Now, where does he keep the toolbox?

The grass was so long because she has been away for the month of May. You can't let the grass grow for the month of May and expect anything other than a hayfield. She's been in Finland; she's not sure why. Since this time last year she has travelled to all the countries Elk had ever lived in, or loved. Four or five. There have been various reasons for going to the different countries: a book launch, a sixtieth birthday party, a conference. A funeral. But there was always another reason under the surface, always exactly the same reason. Dreams have an overt narrative, which usually repeats random bits and pieces of your recent conscious experience, and a latent one, a broken record churning out the same old message for all of your life. Apparently her waking life is now operating on the same principle as her dream life.

This doesn't particularly surprise her.

Why travel? To get away from Elk, on the one hand, and to look for him, on the other. Why else go to his places, far-flung northern islands and archipelagos, rather than perfectly nice warm countries that might cheer her up? The only reason for the choice, which seemed not like a choice, was that he might be far away in the north, hidden in the deep evergreen forest, or sitting on the edge of a lake, fishing for pike? Or climbing the side of a volcano?

Maybe he's here, in the south of Ireland, in the cottage in Kerry, in the library, or sitting on the side of the ancient volcano at the back of the house, looking out at the Great Blasket?

The red toolbox is in the corner at the back, hidden behind an old dustbin. She takes out a screwdriver and tightens the loose nut. When she is replacing the tool in the box, something catches her eye.

A bottle of wine.

Empty?

No. It's a Chablis. 2007.

They must have bought it one year – 2008? – on the way down, from the farm shop in Nenagh where they often stopped for a coffee, and to buy treats. Cheese from France, country butter from Tipperary. Mango chutney with caramelised onions that somebody in Cloughjordan makes. Mostly they drank the wine on the first night. But he must have tucked this one away in the garage for a special occasion and forgotten about it.

Or maybe she did that herself.

Once a year he wanted to drive to Brandon Creek; often on a Sunday afternoon when there was that Sunday-afternoon feeling, that mix of nostalgia (for what? For nothing you can put your finger on) and boredom. The sound of football commentaries, wildly excited, from car windows and cottage windows, which filled Frida with a strange ennui, a longing to escape to somewhere, she knew not where, even when she was eight years old. One of the great things about Elk was that he couldn't care less about football, didn't even know that that was an unusual gift, in a man.

But even so.

Let's go to Brandon Creek.

Cuas an Bhodaigh. St Brendan is supposed to have sailed from there, in a *naomhóg* and landed in America. Who knows? He could have landed in Iceland, like the monks from Teelin. But there is another tale associated with it, and that's what drew Elk to it. The story of the Big Bodach, a sea man who came sweeping in from the ocean and made love to a woman who was swimming there. Raped? But she fell in love with him; she went down to the water every day to meet him, so it was not rape, apparently. This woman had been married for seven years, but had no child. When the deed was done the water man walked back into the water and she never saw him again. But nine months later she gave birth to a son who was half human and half merman, as only she knew. The son had a problem: he could never sleep.

'The Devil's Son as Priest', it's called in the international index of tales. Although he's not a devil; just not human. Not someone you should be consorting with.

Reading it for the tenth time, it occurred to her that the man from the sea may be the father-in-law of the woman. The story may be about incest. She never noticed this aspect until now. You see something new, every time you read a story, if it is any good.

One thing she often noticed: nobody went for a swim in Brandon Creek. It's a long narrow inlet, a fjordful of black water, fathoms deep, a ravine, a chasm, loomed over by Mount Brandon at the back and by black cliffs on each side. The creek crashes angrily down into the fjord, and the water slurps ominously into eerie crevices in the rock. There's no beach of any kind.

It's like an entrance to another world – and not a very nice one, if the gateway is anything to go by. You can understand that Brendan, obviously fond of high drama, would sail from here to the unknown, in mythology, and that a big *bodach* from beneath the wave, a merman, Neptune, would emerge here. Here, rather than some golden sandy cove or long stretch where children play in the frilly shallows and where any normal woman would go for her dip.

Frida parks the car high above the creek, in a sort of lay-by, and walks down a winding boreen to the water. A young couple are on the way up, the girl with long black hair, the boy a redhead. They are dancing up the road, laughing, waltzing and humming like bees in the sunshine. Or two butterflies. They don't see her at all, have eyes only for one another.

At the start of the pier Kerry County Council has a warning: Do Not Enter This Pier if the Sea is High. DANGEROUS. The sea isn't high, on this fine summer's evening. Down to the end of the pier she goes. There's a car parked on it. People drive the whole way down sometimes; it always amazes her. They hate walking so much, they'd rather risk drowning. A man in a navy blue jumper. Hello. A bit cheeky. Lovely day. She doesn't look at his face, but walks to the end and looks down into the water. It's not black when you're beside it. Transparent. Seaweed, and fishes, a flip-flop or something thrown away.

Behind her, she can sense the man in the blue jumper.

His eyes on her back.

She becomes conscious of how lonely it is here, at Cuas an Bhodaigh. She's alone at the end of a pier, with deep black water all around. This happens, a lot. She's in a place she likes on her own, and she suddenly feels, I shouldn't be here. Why am I here?

She turns and goes back along the pier and up the winding hill to her own car.

The man is at the back of his car as she approaches,

doing something in the boot. She walks past, trying to look carefree.

'Here!' he hails her again. She jumps out of her skin. 'Have you any use for crab claws?'

He extends a plastic bag full of them.

'I've more than I need.'

'Thanks,' she takes the bag, and forces a smile. Elk loves crab claws, and so does she.

'A treat for your tea.'

'Thanks!' she repeats. 'We like them. Thanks.'

She walks slowly up the hill. The young couple have disappeared. Before she gets into her car she looks down at the inlet. The man in the blue jumper is reversing, down the slip, towards the water. She can hear it lapping and slapping against the stone, friendly, before it deepens and becomes a dark other world.

They'll have a nice dinner to celebrate the cutting of the grass and the survival of the New Zealand flax. She has the crab claws and the wine. New potatoes and salad and spinach. Lemon, oregano.

She peels the potatoes, puts them on. Slices spring onions and tomatoes; chops parsley. Spreads the white tablecloth, and sets it with the best cutlery she can find. Flowers. Buttercups, clover, and two of the orchids, which may be a protected species but since she has saved the lives of about fifty of them today her guilt is minimal. In the small glass jar they look lovely, against the snow of the cloth. When it gets dark – which won't be till about half past ten – she will light the white candle.

She has Beethoven's Pastorale beside the CD player for when dinner is ready. One of his favourites. One of everyone's favourites. Now she's listening to Kathleen Ferrier's hits although she shouldn't, because it opens with 'Blow the Wind Southerly', a song of longing for a sailor who won't come home, because he is drowned. Blow the wind southerly, southerly, southerly, bring my love safely back home to me. And somewhere on the CD – it is towards the end – is Orfeo's lament for Euridice. What is life if thou art dead? The saddest song in the world. Tradition doesn't hold back on emotion and neither does opera, though few get as close to the bone as Gluck.

She travelled to get away, to look for something, to forget and to remember. But coming home all she wanted was to tell him about her travels. Coming home, she realised that the main point of them was to report them back. Actually, she usually realised that about two days in, but batted away the thought.

Which is why she has invited him to dinner tonight. There were so many aspects of them that only he would want to hear about. She wants to ask him about the loan words, how the Finns seemed to drop the 's' from some words they borrowed from Swedish. *Kuola* from *skole*, for instance. *Tie* instead of *Stig*. And other words that are so strange. He would know why the Finns call a book *kirj*. You'd expect the word for book to come from Latin, or Greek, or Swedish, or even Russian. Where did they get *kirj* from?

Who cares about this sort of stuff?

Elk and Frida.

Into the thick goblets from the local pottery she pours the old wine. Sits down, and raises her goblet.

'*Kippis!*' she says, to the empty chair opposite her.

The Finnish for *sláinte*.

She sips the wine.

'It is very good,' she says. 'I can never sort out what the Finns did during the Second World War. Can you explain? So I get it straight?'

The sun is still high, in the south-west, over the island they call the Dead Man. Frida prefers the other name, the Northern Island.

Euridice! *Eurid eeeeeeche.*

What is life without your love.

At last the sun starts to sink behind the Northern Island. Elk loved it when they showed that scene on RTÉ, back in the days when they played the national anthem at close of programming.

The blue of the night.

And when the sun slides down behind the Dead Man he comes out of the study and sits in his own place at the table.

'Will you have some wine?'

He looks at the bottle as if he has never seen one before. Puzzled, shakes his head.

He looks like himself. Not pale and thin as he was in the last year, or panic-stricken as on the last days in the hospital, with his horribly swollen stomach and tubes shoved down his throat. He's wearing his navy blue jumper, which is odd, because that's the jumper she keeps under her pillow at home in the city.

'Now you're here I don't know what to say to you.'

She leans over to take his hand. His long fingers, thin and agile from a lifetime of typing, like a pianist's. But he pulls it away, not unkindly.

'Well.' She says the first thing that comes to her head. And yet she knows the time is valuable, like the time you've got for a job interview. You've only got half an hour so don't waste it saying unimpressive things. 'I miss you.'

'Yes, my darling.' His voice is his voice. Soft, round, robust, male, like a mellow burgundy. Like a purple orchid. 'Well, I am glad to hear that, even if it is selfish.'

'I miss you a lot.'

No need to repeat yourself.

'Yes, yes. It's terrible.' He sighs. 'But spilt milk.'

'I went to Finland.'

'Good for you! *Puhutekko Suomi?*'

'*Anteeksi! Mina en puhu Suomi.*'

'Good woman!'

'That's all I learnt.'

'Did you have a sauna?'

'Nearly every day. You'd have loved that. We should have got one, for your back.'

He is blurred, like a photograph that is not in focus. Sometimes the photos are like that, on the computer, and then after a little while they swim into clarity.

'I was listening to that song, Euridice.'

'Maybe you could find something more cheerful?'

'I've got Abba's *Greatest Hits* in the car.'

'*Ush!*'

'I cut the grass yesterday. I came down specially to do it. It was over a foot long.'

'My dear little darling.' Nobody ever calls her that any more. She's not even little. 'But you shouldn't come down here just to cut the grass. Why don't you get someone to do it?'

'I will,' she promises.

There is plenty to tell him. About the funeral. About the tributes, the obituaries, the solemn ones and the funny ones. That he has a new grandchild and that their other son is going to get married at the end of the summer. And especially that she has found out how much she loves him, that she always loved him and should have told him that more often. She should have told him that every minute. She needs to tell him these things, and to ask several more practical questions. Where is the article about 'The Dead Lover's Return'? The introduction to the book he was collaborating on with the guy in Galway? Is the Bodach in that story the father-in-law of the woman? What used he do on Sundays, before they were married?

That's before she even gets to the big issue.

'I got a man to level the field.'

He looks out the window. The field is not actually very level. The man came with a digger or a bulldozer or something and dug it up, then put some grass seed in last August. It cost about a thousand euro but nobody has noticed that it is any different from before. Apart from Frida herself.

He walks to the window.

'It's very nice, my darling!'

He doesn't comment on the New Zealand flax. She points its spikes out to him, down by the septic tank. They look like nothing. Like a few rushes that the lawnmower missed.

'They're a bit scrawny but they'll get bigger and make a shelter belt and then I can grow other things.'

'That will be just lovely, won't it?'

He can be ironic and kind at the same time.

There is one thing she really has to tell him. She can't say it so she puts on the CD and the voice comes pouring into the dim room.

'What is life if thou art dead?'

He leans over, and his face is close to her, his woollen jumper.

'Dear darling. I miss you too.' He looks around the room, at the fireplace and the bookshelves and the pictures. 'I miss everything. And there is so much work I didn't get done.' For the first time his face is sad. 'But you don't want to come with me.'

'I do.'

It strikes her that this is the solution. It's simple.

'No, dear darling. You went to Finland. You cut the grass. And you've planted those ... scraggy things!'

'New Zealand flax.'

He laughs.

'Yes, New Zealand flax! You've got to look after the New Zealand flax, and make sure it grows big and beautiful.'

Frida doesn't know why it has that name. It looks nothing like ordinary flax, that rare and beautiful blue corn from which linen is made. New Zealand flax is not blue, and its flowers look like withered prunes. It never flowers in this climate, and looks like a handful of green swords, rusty from the west wind, with pointed tips that cut you if you touch them. There's only one reason for planting it.

'It survived the winter!'

'Yes, my darling, it survived the winter.'

He gets up.

'Don't go.'

Please don't go.

'Yes, I must go. Before the sun rises. You know the rules!'

He walks towards the door.

'The sun won't rise for ages.'

'It has already risen in Finland.'

She runs after him.

'Will you come back?'

He turns.

'One of us had to go first. That's the way it is.'

They warn you. Till death do us part. You hear it but you don't take it in. You throw it away, into the bin, like the wrapping paper on a beautiful present.

He puts a hand towards her shoulder, but not on it. If only he could hold her in his arms for one second!

'Make the most of the time you have left. It will be over soon enough. There's plenty of work to do.' He winks. 'You can do mine, if you don't want to do your own.'

'Yes,' she says. 'I will.'

He always gives good advice.

Imagination is supposed to be a great thing. A gift. It can conjure up, it can invent. But its creations are as nothing, really, compared to the real thing.

The man on the pier didn't reverse into the water. He attached a rope, which was dangling from the back of his car, to a small boat in which he must have been out before she came, fishing or something. And he pulled it up after him, to dry land.

As I Lay Dying

I sometimes imagine that I am dying. I don't mean now. Of course not. Like most people, I assume my death will happen in the distant, unforeseeable, future. In my imagination, I am *old*, much much older than I am at present, and I am on my deathbed. It's in a hospital – I don't know which one but I give myself a private room, clean and white as in the television dramas, and a nubbly bedspread, the kind they have in many hospitals I have visited here, in Ireland, where I live. I'm not attached to drips or machines, although they are in evidence, and I'm not in pain or distress. (I'm giving myself an easy death!) My hair is silver. I'm wearing glasses.

I look to be about eighty-five, ninety, something like that. Comfortably far away.

Also I look quite different – like some old schoolteachers I had when I was eight or nine (they were younger than I am now but they looked ancient). Or like the granny in 'Little Red Riding Hood'. My two sons who are with me, however, look exactly how they look today. Apparently I'm incapable of foreseeing how their appearances will change over the next twenty years, although I have witnessed their changing faces and bodies now for almost forty. But when, how, did these great changes occur? I saw them happen before my eyes, but I can't answer that question.

We aren't chatting. It's not one of those cheery deathbeds you sometimes hear about. Such scenes are hailed with warm approval. 'My dying father asked for a Chinese takeaway and we had a party!' No thanks. I definitely don't want a celebration, where everyone has to perform, pretend to be having a good time – although, who knows, maybe some of them will be feeling happy to see the last of me? (They'll be the last ones to cheer and whoop, in plain sight, you can be sure!) But nor do I envisage one of those gloomy scenes where everyone puts on a funeral face. My elder son is looking at his phone – see, I can't imagine what will replace mobile phones in twenty years either. My other son is just sitting, contemplatively, attentively, as he always does. When I say deathbed I mean I won't be leaving this bed, this hospital – but I'm not kicking the bucket this minute.

Right now we seem to have all the time in the world. I am aware of what is going to happen next. Death. But there's no rush, and there's no appointment. Nobody sets a date or a time. I suspect I will get impatient, if a few days pass and death has still not turned up. What's keeping you? I can't hang around here for ever, just waiting – I haven't reached that stage yet. But it's very possible that my children have. After all, they have lives to get back to, out of this waiting room, this death room. Outside, the show is still going on, as we say, and in here, it gets boring, after a while. Waiting for anything – a plane, a phone call – gets boring. You have to find ways to pass the time, while, deep down, all you want is to board the plane, to get moving to the next place, the next experience.

This would be a good time for a serious family conversation. Not a thing my family ever practised much – it's not that we are unaffectionate or afraid to show our feelings, but deep searching conversations about feelings just aren't our thing. Actually, since something momentous is about to happen, I have made an exception to the convention, and we have already had an economical version of the deathbed conversation. I've told them how much I love them, how proud I am of them. I've told a few amusing but affectionate stories about their childhoods and that sort of thing. I've also been practical and told them about my will, and discussed funeral arrangements. They found it all embarrassing, especially the bit about the funeral … and I don't enjoy thinking about a funeral that I won't be at myself, except in a coffin. Now that is frustrating! I can make all the arrangements I want but I won't see what actually happens; if 'my wishes' are adhered to. And I know it will be all the same to me whether they are or they aren't, because there will be no *me*. Apparently I have no difficulty in accepting that there was no 'me' before I was born. But that I cease to exist after I die is a harder proposition.

Ting a ling. A text. My younger son pulls his phone out of his pocket. He glances at it, then fixes me with his steady gaze and says, neutrally, 'Susan wonders if she can come in to see you.'

I close my eyes.

I feel tired.

This is the way I have often felt, on the bus, going to the theatre to perform, in the evening. Halfway to the venue I feel, deeply, deep in my body, that I do not want to do this thing. Weariness infects me like a rapid dose of anaesthetic. I close my eyes and think that I would so much rather be staying at home, cooking dinner, watching TV, than heading into town to put on a show. But then when I get there and put on my costume, step onto the stage, it's all fine, it's enjoyable, it's great! I used to comfort myself by saying that this reluctance was nerves, butterflies in my tummy, and that without them the show would not be good. I wouldn't perform well. I'm not sure now if there is any truth in that belief. There are so many silly superstitions in the theatre. In life.

Susan.

My sister.

My estranged sister

I should disguise her. As my daughter, my son. My stepdaughter. Hardly my mother or stepmother, since I am eighty-five in this scene. Or ninety. But I can't think of any other relation that would work, in this story. It should be easy to come up with alternatives. The world is full of families at war with one another. Cold war. I know of close relatives who never speak to one another, mothers and daughters, fathers and sons. Siblings. I don't think it's true that there are more families experiencing estrangement than the opposite. But off the top of my head I can count seven in my own circle, which is neither big nor small, just average.

'It's always about money,' my cousin says. His sisters haven't spoken to him in about twenty years. It is often about money – especially money that is not earned, but inherited. It causes resentment in those who don't get it, or don't get enough, or as much as they believe they are entitled to, entitled by virtue of their existence. But other factors play a part. I googled estrangement once to see if there was a common denominator. There isn't. People get angry about all kinds of things (if you can believe what you read on Google) and cut off relations as a response: revenge, punishment, possibly shame at their own outrageous behaviour in the heat of a moment. The guilty find it difficult to forgive those they have injured.

In the case of me and my sister Susan, it may be partly about money, but it is mainly about a cat.

Susan's cat, Puff.

Susan is ten years younger than me. She was born when my mother was already forty, and was perfect and healthy, but always rather small for her age, and, it turned out as time went on, 'delicate' – she often had a cold. So did my mother. And her colds were more serious, although we didn't know that for a long time. Anyway, probably to compensate for the fact that her mother was often in bed, sick, and that Susan had to spend a lot of time alone, she was given a cat.

Not an ordinary cat. A Norwegian Forest cat. He was enormous, because he had an enormous thick fur coat; he looked a bit like Zsa Zsa Gábor, in *Green Acres*, in her enveloping mink, or like a big porcupine, but with soft luxurious brown fur instead of spikes. In the wild, in the mountains of Norway, these cats need their thick water- and snow-proof coats for the cold weather. Puff didn't need it in the place where he spent most of his life: our living room, where he curled up on a sofa or armchair for most of the day and only bestirred himself when it was time to eat. Whatever hunting instincts his ancestors had had deserted him. Puff was one of the world's laziest cats.

When we got him – or when Susan got him: she was

insistent that he was 'her cat' – I wanted to call him Ibsen. But she didn't like that name and decided on Puff.

Puff the Magic Dragon.

Lazy and sweet, as far as Susan was concerned. But he had a little foxy face, buried in his mass of brown fur, which could look gentle and innocent, but turned vicious if he was annoyed in the slightest way. Which happened frequently. He was irritable by nature. His green, almond-shaped eyes would sharpen and he would glare at whoever had angered him, opening his little mouth and baring his pointy teeth, stretching his front legs and showing his claws. At such moments, nature broke through a century of taming and gleamed in his eyes. He had been domesticated – in his case, the word is too weak; he had been bred to a life of luxury like some fat prince in a costume drama – but buried in that furry cushion was a mean feline whose ancestors had survived by systematically slaughtering the beautiful birds, the little woodland creatures of the Nordic forests. (Of course, he never bothered our sparrows or robins or mice, since he had easier ways of getting grub.)

I didn't have to pay a lot of attention to Puff. By the time he took up residence in our house, I was out of it a lot of the time, busy with my life of studying and window shopping and meeting boys.

Whereas, apart from the time she spent at school, Susan was at home all the time, looking after Puff, nursing him on her lap, loving him.

Our mother's cough worsened. And then she died. Not suddenly, but within three weeks of being diagnosed with lung cancer, when I was eighteen and Susan eight.

There is no age – at least not before middle age – at which it is easy to lose your mother. But I have always thought from five or six to twelve must be the worst.

It was easier for me. She died in November when I was in my first year in college. I was deeply involved already with the drama society, which was going to be the training ground for my career – as I already hoped, and more or less knew. I was also deeply in love with my boyfriend – I felt more love for him than I did at that time for my mother, or my father, or Susan, or anyone on this earth. Susan, I dimly divined, was in love with our mother, as little children are. She felt as I would have felt if he – his name was Timmy, a rather silly name, really – had been run over by a bus, or killed in some way.

Then I did lose him. Six months later we split up.

This affected me more than the death of my mother. Much more. (Ridiculous, I know. But it is the truth.) I couldn't accept that he, who had been the centre of my life for a year and a half, was no longer in it. No longer wanted to be in it, no longer loved me. Was, even, in love with somebody else.

I stopped going to college, I stopped going out – I felt everyone could see how miserable I was; what an object of pity, a pathetic soul. Poor thing. She lost her mother and now she's lost her boyfriend. (Most people didn't even know I had a boyfriend, but that's how I felt.) Anyway, the only person I wanted to go out with, to go out to, was him. The person I could not have. Timmy.

I stayed at home, made a half-hearted effort to look after Susan (our dad was back at work a week after the funeral; he was often out at night, in the pub or somewhere). I watched TV.

I had a special chair, as if I were an old lady of seventy. I'd always had it, but before Timmy and I broke up, I hadn't been in it all that often. It was a big old soft yellow chair, near the fireside and with a good view of the TV.

My TV chair. Now, I spent hours and hours of every day and evening in that chair, watching any stupid programme that came on – *The Lucy Show*, *Glenroe*, *The Fugitive*. And I read novels. Classics like those by the Brontës, and new writers like Margaret Drabble; anything that dealt with love and loss interested me.

One evening, after I came in from the kitchen where I'd made beans on toast for Susan, Puff was on my chair.

'Down you get!' I said, knowing he wouldn't move. I lifted him off. He snarled. I settled in to watch the six o'clock news. About an hour later I got up again to go to the loo and when I returned he had taken up residence again.

'He likes your chair,' Susan said.

'I like my chair too. He can sit somewhere else.'

Puff had his own basket, lined with silk cushions. He never lay there.

I moved him to the sofa, where he had often been perfectly happy until his recent whim. His eyes narrowed and he gave me a mean look.

The battle between me and Puff continued for a week. Cat hair got into my chair, and it became smelly – Puff was a clean cat, but still a cat. And he made a point of farting more than was at all necessary when he was in my chair, just to get at me. As soon as I came into the room and approached the chair he'd let out a huge big fart, stinking of cat food and cat wind. Whenever I managed to sit in it, my own chair, I got up feeling catty – with Norwegian Forest cat fur stuck to my clothes and the stink of cat fart under my skin.

Then he actually did a poo. On my chair.

'It's gone far enough, Ibsen!' I picked him up and carried him to the back door.

He squealed and glared, shocked out of his mind. Nobody had ever treated him like this before.

As I put him down on the grass, he extended his paw – he had a long reach – and scratched my face so it bled.

I left him in the garden to let him reflect on his sins.

Meanwhile I went to the little hardware store in our suburban village and asked for rat poison.

'Do you have ID?' The man who ran the shop looked at me curiously. I'd hardly ever been in the shop, although my father was a regular customer.

'No.'

'Sorry,' he said. 'We're not allowed to sell it to anyone under the age of eighteen.

I then went to a bigger hardware store, further from home. I found the section called 'Pesticides'. Shelves of mouse and rat traps, devices for scaring away birds, various kinds of poison for fleas, moths. And rodents. There were several brands. I took packs of three different kinds, just to be on the safe side.

Nobody asked me for ID. The teenager on the checkout didn't in fact look at me or at what I was buying. She seemed to be half asleep as she checked through the items on automatic pilot.

It took two days to poison Puff.

Needless to say, he was a picky eater. From the word go, he had rejected cheap brands of catfood, and only ate the most expensive Whiskas and the other premium tins, which he saw advertised on TV as he sat and dozed. But what he liked best were little tubs of something that looked like liver pâté. That's what Susan insisted on feeding him. I made sure to feed him before Susan got up or came home from school. Each helping of pâté was supplemented by a small dose of poison – I knew he wouldn't eat it if he got a whiff of something suspicious.

Over three days, Puff got tired. He hardly moved at all from my chair. I almost felt sorry for him.

'There's something wrong with him.' Susan was alarmed. She had watched my mother fading away over some years and was inclined to worry.

'He's just a bit tired.'

'He's sick. Let's bring him to the vet.'

'If he's not better by Friday, we will.'

But on Thursday afternoon, just before Susan got in from school, Puff died.

Susan didn't find out about my poisoning of Puff. But she knew I didn't like him (I hated him actually, but she could not even imagine that anyone would.) Intellectually, she didn't suspect me – how could she? She believed Puff to be so adorable that she could not imagine anyone wanting to do anything but cuddle and love him. But somehow, deep inside herself, she knew what had happened. She knew I had done it. Allowed her cat to die.

It was my biggest mistake, in life – the one I regret most.

And still, his death energised me. After Puff's funeral – he was buried with all due ceremony in the garden under an apple tree – my depression or gloom or whatever it was lifted. I got out of bed and washed and dressed in the mornings, and resumed my life. A year later I was playing the lead role in *Lady Macbeth*, Dramsoc's big production that year. (What I mean is, I played Lady Macbeth. The play is called *Macbeth*, as you know.)

Susan never got over Puff. Not in a few weeks, not in a few years. On the contrary, she sank into a peculiar state of depression that lasted for ages. During that time, she hardly spoke to me or to anyone – she didn't become mute, like some children who experience terrible trauma, like girls in fairy tales and myths. But she lost whatever vestige of liveliness she had ever had. From being a quiet child she became a neurotically quiet child, and remained like that as she grew into adolescence and adulthood. Beautiful, with her long black hair, green almond eyes; tall and willowy. But silent.

In spite of her seeming lack of energy, she got through school, did very well in her exams, went to college. She became a vet. And not long after graduating she married quite a nice young man. A writer, who was working on a novel. Not the husband my father – still less my mother – would have desired for either of their daughters, but we were relieved, and surprised, that she married at all. And they had two children. He – Dan, that's his name – had high ambitions and was not without talent. But he lacked something. The drive you need to succeed in the arts world – it's not all about talent. You need luck also. Susan was and remained the breadwinner. (To be fair to him, Dan did all the childcare.)

After her marriage, Susan and I saw less and less of each other. I wrote to her occasionally, inviting her to family gatherings, or asking if she'd like to meet for coffee but she always presented some excuse. And then we saw nothing of each other at all.

That's how estrangements come about, in families. Most of those I have heard about start for much more stupid reasons than the murder of a cat.

The fact is, though, that I didn't love Susan. No. Never. However, maybe that is partly retrospective – since now we have a very bad relationship, no relationship, it's difficult for me to imagine that I could ever have loved her.

And who have I ever really loved? My husband. I loved him. A few other men. I love my own children. I love my grandchildren. I have friends of whom I am very fond, so perhaps I love them, in a way – for the way I can talk to them about anything, for their loyalty. How many kinds of love are there? Eros. That's my husband. Agape. That's friends. And filial and maternal. Susan didn't fit into any of the categories. I suppose that's the problem. Sisterly love. But what she needed was maternal love, from me, and she never got that. I was only a child myself.

When I open my eyes, my older son is bent over me, holding my hand.

'I'm still alive,' I say. 'No worries.'

Someone else has come into the room. She's walking towards the bed, a tall girl in a blue summer frock. Long dark hair.

One of my granddaughters, Louisa. She comes to the deathbed and kisses me. Louisa is thirty years of age. Her father, my son, is already fifty-five. Susan, it occurs to me, is in her seventies. Early eighties. An old old woman. When I last saw her she was not much older than Louisa. I had imagined her still that age, a young woman with long black hair. I wonder what she looks like now. Red Riding Hood's granny?

Now I have a chance to find out. To see her, one more time.

Also, a chance to be forgiving. Noble. Good.

Possibly she has the same idea? About herself? The text. She has made her grand gesture, lobbed the ball into my court.

My usual practice, all my life – my life after Puff – has

been to be forgiving, to forget grudges. What is the point? My husband shared this view. Life is too short, we would say. *Noblesse oblige*. We were, to be honest, a little smug about our attitude; we felt superior.

Susan estranged herself from me; I had been willing to change that, for decades.

But now, as I lie dying, it seems that I have been changed too, and not for the better. I've transformed into one of those people who do not forgive or forget. Worn down, bitter, clinging to their grudges as if they were comforting pillows, soft old teddy bears, which they won't let go of, even as they let go of life itself.

I'm not going to die today, and probably not tomorrow either. I've eaten something today – some consommé, a little fruit salad. I'm sipping water. Usually dying people don't eat anything, or drink anything. A woman I trust told me that, a nurse. When they stop eating, that's The Sign.

I say, 'Can you play some music?'

My younger son looks startled.

'Yes. What?'

'Something that I like. "The Dance of the Happy Shades". "Going Home".'

I trust him to find exactly the right thing.

He chooses something by Grieg, from *Peer Gynt*. The big round puffs of romantic sound fill the room. 'Morning Mood'. And oh, I am in Norway on the side of a mountain, not doing anything in particular. Just wandering along a winding path through the high evergreen trees, walking towards the rising sun.

ACKNOWLEDGEMENTS

Some of these stories have been previously published in the *Irish Times*; Belinda McKeon (ed.), *A Kind of Compass* (Dublin, Tramp Press, 2015); Dimitar Kambourov (trans.), *A Literary Lunch and Other Stories* (Sofia, ICU, 2018); and Maria Teresa Casal and Ana Raquel (eds), *Home* (Lisbon, 2020).

Thanks also to the Baltic Centre for Writers and Translators on Gotland, to the Tyrone Guthrie Centre in Annaghmakerrig, and to the International Summer School in Veliko Tranovo, Bulgaria, where some of these stories were written.

As always, my heartfelt thanks to one of the world's best editors, Patsy Horton at Blackstaff Press. I would also like to thank my ever-supportive family – siblings, children, and grandchildren – especially my son Ragnar, my biggest fan.

Twelve Thousand Days: A Memoir of Love and Loss
Éilís Ní Dhuibhne

'A precise and honest self-portrait, carefully crafted
… absorbing and moving.'
Colm Tóibín

'Éilís Ní Dhuibhne uses all her lyricism to pay
tribute to the relationship that defined her being.'
Eileen Battersby

'A love story in all its human complications and
shared moments of quiet.'
Dermot Bolger

'Stark and moving and a masterclass in structure.'
Sarah Gilmartin